COVER ME IN CHOCOLATE

Fetish Alley Series – Book 3

Susan Mac Nicol

ALSO BY SUSAN MAC NICOL

THE STARLIGHT SERIES
Cassandra by Starlight
Together in Starlight
Forever in Starlight

THE MEN OF LONDON SERIES
Love You Senseless
Sight & Sinners
Suit Yourself
Feat of Clay
Cross to Bare
Flying Solo
Damaged Goods
Hard Climate
Survival Game
Not So Secret Santa

FETISH ALLEY SERIES
For Fox Sake
Death By C*ck

OTHER TITLES
Stripped Bare
Saving Alexander
Worth Keeping
Double Alchemy
Double Alchemy: Climax
Love and Punishment
Sight Unseen
Unlikely in Love
Living On Air
Soul of Discretion
Promises Kept

www.BOROUGHSPUBLISHINGGROUP.com

COVER ME IN CHOCOLATE

ISBN 978-1-951055-30-1

To all my wonderful readers who have given me endless pleasure with their support, kind words, and funny memes on social media. I appreciate every single one of you so much. You keep me going when I feel I'm flapping in the wind heading nowhere.

ACKNOWLEDGMENTS

Huge thanks to new family members, Laura Munro and her husband James. They were amazing in helping me with the research for the police procedure used in this book. Any errors are completely my own.

To my day job boss and former chocolatier, Ralph, thanks for the tips and clarifications on this intriguing and tasty process.

Ann Alaskan, my lovely friend on the other side of the pond, as always thanks for your wisdom and insight into the psychological aspects of my stories and the character development. The same hearty thanks goes to Kirsty Bicknell and Jack L Pyke for their invaluable input and sensitivity reading. I hope Joshua comes across as I intended, and I leave readers to make their own assumptions about why he behaves as he does. I wasn't going to put a label on him.

All the foreign language used in the book, a mix of Italian, Lithuanian, and Russian, I checked out with people who spoke the language in the necessary forums. Once again, any errors made are entirely my own.

The Fetish Alley series is on hold for now. I feel the need to do something different. I adore Tate and Clay but I need a change from writing a series. Watch for the Valentine's story coming your way in February, and the rock-star romance that will drum its way to you sometime in 2020. I may feel the need to write something else in between too. Perhaps a cozy mystery or a NA fantasy novel. We'll see where the muse takes me.

COVER ME IN CHOCOLATE

Chapter 1

There was something comforting about the man sitting across from her. He was polite and attentive, and it was lovely being treated like a princess. Olivia sighed softly. It'd been a while since she'd gone on a friend date—two people meeting, seeing something likeable in each other and agreeing to have a drink together.

She needed a friend right now and the man refilling her wine glass could become one. He'd been so sweet to her in the past. The tiny squirming worm of unease in her stomach niggled at her. She knew her current boyfriend, Allan, wouldn't like her being in this cosy apartment with another man. She shivered at the thought, and her dinner companion cocked his head curiously.

"Are you cold? Would you like another bar on the fire?" His darting gaze regarded her as he made a move to stand up, no doubt to adjust the settings on the small heater sitting on the hearth.

Olivia shook her head. "Oh no, it's fine. A goose walked over my grave, that's all." She pushed all thoughts about her boyfriend away. Allan and his sharp tongue was, no doubt, at home in front of the television. Tonight was Olivia's refuge, her little adventure about which she'd have to lie the next time she saw Allan.

The heat in the room was making her a little drowsy. Her head felt fuzzy, and she blinked, trying to keep her eyes open. The room swam a little and the face of the man sitting across from her at the small dining table blurred.

"I think perhaps I need to stop drinking that lovely wine," she said, wondering why her words were slurred. She wasn't that drunk, was she? She'd only had one glass. "It's going to my head."

He motioned to the couch. "Perhaps you should sit over there, and you can get more comfortable. Let me help you."

Despite her protests, he escorted her from the easy chair to the couch. She was grateful. Her legs *were* rather unsteady. It would be nice to put them up.

"I'll get you a glass of water," her dinner companion said. His voice sounded far away, and Olivia blinked, trying to focus on his words.

The couch was so comfy and warm, and all she wanted to do was close her eyes for a minute and think about what a nice time she'd had tonight away from Allan, away from all the stress and the pain.

She hadn't relaxed like this in ages but somewhere at the back of her brain, an alarm was ringing. *Perhaps I'm stupid trusting someone I barely know*, she thought dreamily, watching the golden flicker of the flames in the hearth. But she'd decided she must take a chance since she wanted to meet new people.

Soft hands were in her hair, brushing it away from her face, touching her tenderly, and it was the last thing she remembered as she sank into sleep with a smile on her face.

***

Darkness seeped across the quiet urban street, shrouding once familiar landmarks in an obsidian cloak, turning the familiar to the unknown in one slow moving sweep of deep shadows.

Tate wrinkled his nose in disgust. He stood next to the back entrance of a now silent Thai restaurant, its structure backlit by the few remaining globes in the stream of lights around its roof. He held back retching from the odour of fish and rotten remnants of patrons' food. The smell of shit exacerbated the stench, drifting over from somewhere further down the alley. Tate didn't know where it was coming from, probably a misbehaving drain. He and his colleague, Ellis Tremont, stood in the deep, dark recesses of one of the most deprived areas of Weston Super Mare in North Somerset. They were there to collect a man known to them only as Smokey D, and escort him to Bristol where he'd be a witness in a murder trial.

The house they were watching was a static home that Smokey D owned on the sly. It sat about forty feet from them, surrounded by gardening implements, broken bits of metal and machinery, and, for some incongruous reason, a broken stone statue of Michelangelo's David.

There'd been a text message from the Welsh team earlier advising Tate the pickup was on for tonight. Smokey D would meet them at ten pm. The tell-tale sign he was home would be a double flash of the porch light from the static home.

Beside him, Ellis breathed shallowly through his mouth, his puffs forming steamy clouds in the air. "I don't know how I got myself into this situation," he muttered peevishly. "I'm an inside man, a geek, not a bloody He-Man like you." He took a deep sniff as he talked, and his face twisted in disgust. "God, that smell," he exclaimed. "When you said you were taking me to Somerset on a case, I had visions of beaches and sea air. Not this...." he threw out his hand, "revolting shit." He went back to his careful mouth breathing.

"I didn't say this would be a jolly holiday, Ell," Tate muttered with some amusement. "We're picking up a witness in a bloody gang murder case, not an Agatha Christie villain." The one caveat Smokey D had demanded was no police involvement at this stage of the game. Hence the reason the private investigation firm, Mortimer & Williams, of which Tate was the Williams partner, were the escorts. Tate zipped his hoodie further up as the November wind blew an unexpected gust. "And you brought this on yourself, Ell. Telling Clay you wouldn't mind getting a little more hands-on was a death knell, mate."

"Yes, well, I didn't think it would be this soon, and not as dire as escorting some guy who witnessed a murder." Ellis's teeth chattered, and he swore softly.

"Execution," Tate said absently, watching the house. He thought he'd seen someone lurking around the side of it. "Cold-blooded and well-executed if you'll pardon the pun. Unfortunately, no one planned on Smokey D being in the wrong place at the right time. The best-laid plans, right?"

Ellis shivered and snuggled deeper into his parka. "Christ, it's as cold as Jack Frost's cock."

Tate couldn't hold back an explosive snort of laughter. "That's original. I'll borrow that saying, I think." He squinted, trying to determine if the figure he'd seen earlier was real.

"It would have been nice to have Carzilla here." Ellis smirked in between shivers, referring to the custom-made surveillance van. "You need to tell me how the van got that name. I understand it's a private joke between you and the boss?"

Tate grinned. "Yeah, and he'll kill me if I tell you how the name happened. So don't ask."

"Instead, we have a Hyundai." Ellis's nose wrinkled in distaste. "At least it has tinted windows so nobody can see my shame." He sniffed in disdain.

"You're a snob, you know that?" Tate teased. "It's a car with a heater, and all we need to do is pick up the guy and get him back to the powers that be so they can get him wherever he needs to go."

Tate hoped it would happen soon. This wasn't his idea of a great place to spend time, and he wanted to get home to Clay and a glass of good whisky. The local bar was as clueless as fuck when it came to decent drinks.

Ellis nudged him. "Do you think this guy will show up or are we wasting our time again?" Last night they'd waited until almost two a.m. in the same alleyway waiting for Smokey D to pitch up. Some miscommunication with the Welsh team's information last night had left their plan high and dry.

Tate scowled. "I fucking hope so. I'm freezing my balls off and my hip flask is empty." He and Ellis had drained the last of the gut-warming whisky about twenty minutes ago. It had been a long night.

Ellis sniggered. "First world problems, hey? All I've got is some chewing gum. Fancy a bit?" He reached into the voluminous pockets of his parka and drew out a tattered, grubby bit of silver foil.

Tate looked at it and winced. "I'll pass, thanks." He stiffened as a light flickered from the home they were watching. "He's there. Did you see that?" The light flashed on again and rapidly went off.

"Uh-huh," Ellis said indistinctly as he chewed his gum. "Let's go get him, tiger."

They walked toward the dim light of the dwelling, Tate's fists tight and ready for any signs of trouble. He had an illegal taser in his right front jacket pocket, which he hoped he wouldn't have to use. It was a remnant from his days on the force. He doubted anyone would rat on him for using it if he needed to take down any bad guys. Self-preservation and saving face was probably more important than accusing an upstanding private citizen of taser tag.

"The light went on and off again," Ellis observed as he strode forward. "Looks like our man is eager to get on the road."

The light flickered again, off and then stayed on, the front of the house backlit by a yellow tinge of brightness. Tate frowned.

"Something's not right," he muttered. "I have a bad feeling about this. Slow down a bit, Ell. I want to wait it out."

Ellis stopped immediately and the two men stood silently, puffs of white air forming little clouds before them. Tate's finely tuned sixth sense said in situations like this, the best thing to do was stop and take stock. His instinct for trouble had saved his life many times.

A shadow moved behind a closed curtain in one of the front rooms, and Ellis stepped forward. "That must be him." He stopped as Tate reached out an arm across Ellis's chest and held him back.

"I said stay here," Tate growled. "There are two people in that house. That wasn't the plan."

Ellis stared at Tate, eyes wide. "I only saw one shadow."

Tate shook his head. "Trust me. I saw two, and they were different shapes and sizes." His eyes narrowed as true enough, a second shadow flitted across the curtain.

Ellis gasped. "Go you, Night Hawk. What do you think is happening in there?"

Tate frowned and cracked his neck from side to side. It made a clicking sound and Ellis winced. "Christ, that sounds like the neck of an eighty-year-old, my friend. Remind me to get you a spa day for your birthday. Sounds like your body needs it."

Tate huffed. "That's what happens when you live a life of taking down the bad guys. I can't remember how many times someone has punched me in the face." He squinted at the house, seeing no more shadows. "Looks like whoever was in there has left, not sure what that says about our pickup. My balls are still tingling. Something's still off."

"Your balls tell you when something's not right?" Ellis teased as they moved a few cautious paces forward, and he followed Tate's lead. "Wow, I can't wait to tell Clay –"

Tate never found out what Ellis intended telling Tate's fiancé because at that moment, the house exploded.

Heat washed over Tate, together with dust, debris and a myriad of sharp objects that stung his skin like slivers of steel. Faintly, he heard Ellis's shout of fear or pain as Tate hurtled through the air, landing flat on his back on something unforgiving and rigid. His head snapped backward and forward and for one excruciating second, Tate thought, *and this is why my neck is fucking screwed.*

Then everything faded into a black velvety hole and as much as Tate tried to stay conscious, the effort was futile.

***

"Tate, buddy, wake up." Hands slapped Tate's face, and he gasped in panic as something cold and wet splashed onto his face, seeping into his mouth. "Are you okay?"

Tate opened his eyes to see Ellis's anxious face peering down at him. "What the fuck did you throw on me?" He shook his head, regretting it the second he did as it threatened to rupture his brain. He struggled up, Ellis's hands under his armpits, and glared at his friend.

Ellis didn't look too roughed up. He had grazes and scratches on his cheek, showing pink against the white of his skin. He blinked owlishly. "I still had a bottle of water in my jacket pocket. I thought it might help wake you up. How do you feel?"

"Like the fucking Wicked Witch of the West when the house landed on her," Tate snarled.

"Uhm, you mean the Wicked Witch of the East," Ellis offered unhelpfully. "It was a bucket of water that destroyed The Witch of the West." He chuckled weakly and Tate didn't miss the underlying tension in his voice.

"I don't give a fuck either way." Tate checked himself gingerly. He seemed to be in one piece except for a huge egg on the back of his head and his limbs and bones feeling as bruised as all hell. "Are you okay?"

Ellis nodded. "You caught most of the blast range, and hit the dumpster hard," his voice caught, and he cleared his throat, "I thought you were a goner. I wasn't sure how to explain that to Clay."

His legs gave way and Tate caught him. He helped the trembling man to a sitting position on the ground then sat down carefully next to him as they surveyed the smouldering ruins of the house. People flocked to the area, shouting and giving instructions to stand clear while someone called the Fire Brigade.

Fuck. That's one witness who won't be making it to the witness stand. Tate sighed heavily and brushed debris from his hair. His cheek stung and he wasn't surprised to see his hand come away wet with blood. *Clay will pitch a fit when he sees me.*

Tate looked over at Ellis who sat staring with a fixed blank gaze at the unfolding events. Tate patted Ellis's back awkwardly. Ellis was a desk man, and this was probably the first time they had exposed him to anything of this sort.

"You all right, Ell?" Tate questioned quietly. "I don't want you going into shock. Tell me if you feel weird or anything."

Ellis nodded jerkily. "There were two human beings in that house," he whispered. "They must be dead, mustn't they? I mean, no one could survive a blast like that."

Tate nodded grimly. "I doubt it. Hopefully, when they do the fire investigation, they'll find the two bodies."

Ellis looked at him, eyes red-rimmed. "You think one of them might have got out of that?" He gestured toward the ruins with a shaking hand.

Tate shrugged. "Could be the second guy was the one who had the place blown up and scarpered out of there before it did. Who knows? Nothing surprises me in this game."

He dug into his pocket to find his mobile, scowling when he saw the shattered state of it. There was no way he'd be calling Clay.

"Your phone working?" he asked Ellis.

Ellis dug in his jacket then gave an apologetic grimace. He held up a phone with a cracked screen. "Nope. It's in the same condition as yours. I think I fell on it."

A paramedic hustled over to them and crouched down. "You guys all right? You look a bit battered."

Tate shrugged and winced at the pain radiating through his back and shoulders. "I'm good. My friend here might need a bit of TLC though. It's his first time being blown up." It heartened him to hear Ellis' amused snort.

The paramedic, a young woman with deep red hair, raised an eyebrow. "You think? You have blood everywhere. Your face is cut to ribbons and you're rolling those shoulders. Something tells me you're in more pain than you let on." She snorted. "Bloody men and their macho rubbish."

Her no-nonsense tone made Tate blink in surprise. Ellis sniggered. "She's got you down pat. Let the lady look you over, for God's sake. I'll take the next turn."

The paramedic–she introduced herself as Emily–fiddled about with her kit and before long, Tate found himself patched up, two butterfly plasters on his cheek, another bandage on his arm concealing a large, nasty gash he hadn't even known was there.

"The lump on your head seems okay, but you could have a concussion," she observed as she pressed gentle fingers against his scalp.

"Wouldn't be the first time," Tate muttered. "I know what to look out for, and I'll keep an eye out as will Ellis here." He cast a wry glance at his partner who nodded earnestly.

She'd tut-tutted when Tate had lifted his shirt to reveal a spate of dark bruising. She'd been more concerned about the ones on his back, where apparently there was an imprint of the lid of the dumpster splayed across his middle back.

Christ, no wonder he felt like shit. Emily said nothing about the existing scars on his back and front for which he was grateful. He wasn't in the mood to explain them.

"Not much we can do about the bruising," she murmured as she moved over to tend to Ellis. "But if you see blood in your pee or have any adverse side effects, get to a hospital immediately." Ellis fared better. He had cuts and bruises on his torso, but nothing that needed too much repair.

When she finished, she stood up and regarded them both thoughtfully. "Earlier, I heard the police wanted to question the two of you. I held them off so I could fix you up first. But I think after I leave, you'll have company."

Tate rolled his eyes, and shit, even that hurt. "I have no doubt," he said drily. He'd seen the two policemen waiting in the distance, casting stern glances over at him and Ellis. "Thanks for the heads up."

Emily turned and left, and no sooner had she gone, then the two cops started to make their way over.

Tate tilted his head toward them. "Incoming," he muttered under his breath. "Let's give 'em what they want and find a phone and call Clay. If he hears about this on the news first, he'll be mightily pissed."

Chapter 2

Aurelio smoothed the lapel of his suit, taking one last glance in the full-length mirror running along half of his bedroom wall. The other half was taken up by a built-in cupboard where he housed his suit collection.

"What do you think of this tie?" he murmured as he fiddled with the knot of the light blue silk dotted with tiny dove grey polka dots. "Do you think this one goes better with this suit or should I wear the grey one?"

The young man sitting cross-legged on Aurelio's bed, laptop open in front of him, looked up, his bright blue gaze lighting on Aurelio's throat.

Tomas Pavlis shrugged. "It looks fine, Relio," he muttered, his faint Eastern European accent as always sexy and inviting. "I don't know why you ask me things like that because you know I'm no fashion guru. If you like it, then that's all that is required." He returned to his laptop.

"*Santa cielo*, Tomas," Aurelio sighed in exasperation. "I am not asking you to become a fashionista, simply asking your opinion on one item. I'll stick with the blue one." Once again, he adjusted the knot until satisfied it lay perfectly.

"This dinner tonight, will it be a late one?" Tomas peered at Aurelio from under a sweep of dark brown hair. It fell over his eyes and he brushed it away absently.

Aurelio loved the new look and preferred the lush head of hair over the shaven head Tomas had sported when they'd first met. The long-sleeved tee-shirt he wore rode up revealing an intricately tattooed sleeve on his right arm. Aurelio knew those tattoos intimately. They were one of his favourite things to kiss and lick.

"It's a dinner with the Chairman of the Chamber of Commerce, who is a dick, so yes, the likelihood is that he will talk until the sheep come home and be as boring as fuck. However, I am hoping to entice him to invest in the Alley's infrastructure, so I will have to grin and bear it."

"Cows," Tomas stated absently.

Aurelio blinked. "What?"

Tomas sighed. "The saying is 'until the cows come home,' not the sheep." He flashed a wicked grin at Aurelio. "I love it when you say stuff like that. It makes you human."

Aurelio glared at his lover. "I am human. What on earth do you mean?"

Tomas uncurled himself from the pretzel position he'd been in hunched over his laptop and knee-walked over to the bottom of the bed where Aurelio stood. "Don't go getting any ideas about a quick blow job," he warned as his hands reached out to encircle Aurelio's hips, his mouth almost level with Aurelio's crotch. "We don't have time for that. All I was saying is you are always so controlled and driven and it's nice to see you too are fallible sometimes. As I said, it makes you human, like the rest of us."

Aurelio reached down and caressed the soft hair on Tomas's head. He loved the way Tomas wore it, heavy on top, short on the sides. "*Tesoro*, you say the strangest things sometimes. I think I have proven to you time and time again that I am quite human." He chuckled at Tomas's eye roll. "And I assure you, tomorrow I have nothing planned and we can spend the whole day together. Unless you made other arrangements."

Tomas was fiercely independent, and while he stayed over at the apartment attached to Graffiato Animé more than he did at his own, Aurelio was under no illusions that his sexy, fiery alley cat wouldn't wander off if the mood took him.

Their relationship was typically tempestuous, but right now they seemed to be in a good place with each other.

Tomas shook his head. "I have some work to do in the morning for Tate but other than that, I am yours all day."

Aurelio liked the sound of that. He bent down and kissed Tomas hungrily on the lips, moving away before it could become too heated, because, well, kisses for them often turned into full-blown sex. "*Amore mio*, you tempt me with those lips, and eyes like the ocean. I think I should leave now before I decide to stay." Reluctantly, he moved away and picked up his jacket, draped over the modern armchair under the window. "I shall see you later.

Behave yourself, and please don't lose any more money to Cleaver in your silly poker game. I have told you he is a cheat and a thief, and yet still you insist on playing with him."

Tomas grinned, showing a flash of white teeth. "But Cleaver is so much fun and he has so many stories to tell. I love listening to him while we play."

Aurelio frowned. "He is also a consummate card shark born in the depths of hell. Heed my warning before you lose your soul to the man." He knew he sounded rather dramatic but as he consoled himself knowing he was an Italian man now living with the cold, rigid British.

Tomas laughed loudly. "Oh, come on, *meilužė*, Cleaver is not the devil." He paused, forehead wrinkling adorably. "Well, perhaps he was back in Jamaica, being mixed up in all that Obeah witchcraft stuff and the gangs, but over here, he's the chief honcho and a bouncer of your club."

Aurelio snorted and picked up his wallet, slipping it into his inside pocket. "Do not underestimate him. That's all I can say."

Tomas got off the bed and prowled over to Aurelio. "You look handsome," he murmured, his fingers skipping down Aurelio's cheek, leaving trails of fire that not only ignited Aurelio's skin but his belly. "Have fun and I shall be in bed waiting when you get back."

Aurelio pulled Tomas to him and for a while he lost himself in Tomas's lips and his scent, the soft spice of his cologne, and the sly slick tongue of his, pressing deep inside Aurelio's mouth. Finally, he knew he had to leave before he'd have to change his suit pants and choose a whole new outfit.

"*Mio caro*, I think it is you that is the devil," Aurelio said huskily when he pulled away. He adjusted himself and walked toward the door. "I will see you later and we can finish what we started."

The soft sound of Tomas's satisfied laughter followed Aurelio out of the room.

***

Tomas leaned back against the crisp cotton sheets of Aurelio's king-size bed and huffed. It was always fun to tease Relio, but not so much fun when left with a dick that was hard and only his hand to ease the urge. He'd much prefer Relio's mouth or strong hands around it, bringing him to the peak of climax, as only Relio could. The man was adept at playing Tomas's body like no other.

Tomas's hand wandered down to his cock and he stroked it idly, closing his eyes, imagining his lover was still there and giving him a blowjob, which he did spectacularly. In his mind, Relio stared up at him, his dark chestnut eyes boring into Tomas's soul as his lips stretched wide around Tomas's girth and Relio's tongue played havoc on his weeping slit. That masterful tongue that could suck and tighten and do things to his cock that led Tomas into the realms of pleasure until all he could do was come, and come, and then lie sated and boneless on the bed.

Tomas's hand tightened around his cock and he moaned, the sound reverberating in the room, as he jacked himself harder, imagining Relio pushing into him, filling his hole with his beautiful dick, so far inside he could taste him.

Spurts of warm come jetted over Tomas's hands and belly, as his body spasmed with the force of his orgasm. He might have shouted out. He wasn't sure. He surrendered his body to the bed, lying blissfully satisfied among the crumpled sheets.

"See what you missed?" he whispered into the room. "You should have stayed to see me come all over myself. I know you love seeing that. Me wet and sticky from all our fluids."

Tomas closed his eyes and gave in to the relaxation of his body and his brain. He fell asleep within minutes.

His mobile phone ringing woke him from a dream where he appeared to be a Sultan in a billowing white tent. More interesting though were the naked men swarming all over him, touching every bit of his body with sly fingers and mouths. Some of them were especially creative and he swore he felt a soreness in his arse he hadn't gone to bed with.

Tomas reached for his phone on the bedside table and barked, "Yes?" because, truly, that dream had been epic and he was sure he'd been about to get to second base with a couple of the men. His skin still tingled with the remnants of the touches to his body.

"Tomas? I'm sorry, did I wake you up?" Tanvi's voice was apologetic. "I thought you'd be up."

Tomas glanced at the time on his phone. Ten p.m. He would normally have been up, being an inveterate night owl, but that orgasm had taken it out of him. "I'm here," he grumbled. "What is up?"

Tanvi was one of his favourite people, other than Cleaver. She was sweet, no-nonsense, treated Relio with respect, and on top of it all, she owned one of the most successful shops in the alley, Chocerotica. It was Tomas's favourite establishment, being a bit of a chocoholic himself.

"I am concerned about Olivia. She hasn't been into work for two days and I can't get hold of her. I wondered if she'd said anything to you about not coming in?"

Tomas frowned. Olivia du Preez was a cute shop assistant at Chocerotica. She and Tomas had struck up a friendship, one that Tomas enjoyed, especially since he didn't make friends easily.

"No, I haven't heard from her." He sat up properly, sheets pooling around his waist. "I came into the shop the day before yesterday and noticed she wasn't there. I thought it might have been her day off."

"No, she had the day off on Thursday but was supposed to work yesterday and today. I tried her mobile a few minutes ago, and this afternoon after work I even knocked on the door of her flat, and still there's been no reply." Tanvi's voice faltered. "I was thinking of doing a welfare check because we all know that prick of a boyfriend has a temper. I called him, but he told me to fuck off, he hasn't seen her. I don't want to embarrass her, what should I do?"

Tomas sighed. "Right. Allan is a wanker. I suppose he could have hit her again." Both Tanvi and Tomas had tried to make Olivia see sense about her awful boyfriend but for whatever reason, Olivia was strangely resistant to their pleas to break up with him. "I'd suggest asking the police to do a welfare check. She wouldn't mind. You're only looking out for her."

"I suppose so. Part of me hopes that she's there, electing not to answer the door, because if she isn't, what's the alternative?" Tanvi sounded close to tears.

"Let's do one thing at a time." Tomas soothed. "See how the welfare check pans out, and then we can take it from there. I'll keep my phone on in case. Let me know either way."

"Okay, Tomas. I'll call the police now and see what they say. I'll call you back if there's any news." Tanvi sounded marginally better at having a plan. "Speak to you later."

The phone went dead and Tomas looked down at his mobile. "That's not like you, Livvy," he murmured. "I promise, if that bastard has done anything to you, I'll ruin him." To be honest, he'd offered to do it before, to wipe Allan's credit history, and embed some illegal activity on his computer for the police to find after a quick and anonymous tip had been sent to their offices. Livvy had laughed, her face strained, and told Tomas that absolutely wasn't necessary, but thank you for caring.

Tomas pursed his lips as he laid down his mobile. Olivia wasn't known for being unreliable or flighty. To learn she'd been gone for two days was worrying.

He narrowed his eyes at his laptop. He supposed he might track her via her telephone number – he had it, as they'd texted each other often about chocolate recipes – and perhaps ping the phone to see where it was. However, as much as Tomas didn't care what he did to make villains' lives miserable, he drew the line at stalking his friends.

But she might be in trouble, the little devil on his shoulder said smugly. Isn't that reason enough to see if I can find her?

She might want some time away on her own and not appreciate anyone searching for her, the angel on his other shoulder remonstrated primly. Are you ready to invade her privacy this way?

He reached up and tugged on his hair in frustration. "Shit," he muttered. "I suppose I'd better wait for the results of the welfare check before I investigate further." He thumped the bed cover moodily. "That fucking boyfriend of hers had better not have done anything to her. I swear, if he has, he'll find out what it means to have never been born. I will erase every trace of him."

Tomas put on his earphones, clicked on his Spotify link and immediately the sounds of his favourite heavy metal rock band, Aunty Acid, blared into his eardrums. He clicked a few keys and was soon lost in his exploration of some off-shore accounts he was researching.

His stomach rumbled as he printed out the last page of a corporate hierarchy for the folder he intended giving to Tate for their case tomorrow. In the distance, in another room, the printer clattered and whirred.

He climbed out of bed, scratching his stomach, and meandered naked through to the kitchen. The clock on the wall caught his eye. It was almost midnight. Relio was having a late meeting. Usually, he wasn't this late.

Tomas opened the fridge and drew out all the ingredients he'd need to make a decent ham and chicken sandwich. Once he'd finished preparing it, he sat down at the table in the polished chrome kitchen and ate his midnight snack with gusto, accompanied by a glass of ice-cold milk.

As he finished the last morsel of bread, he heard the apartment door click open. Tomas grinned and pushed his chair back from the table. He spread his legs and sat there, balls and cock exposed, his legs stretched out.

Might as well give Relio a pleasant surprise, he thought wickedly. Keys hit the hall table, and there was the shuffle of shoes as Aurelio no doubt toed them off. He had a thing about wearing shoes in the flat, worried that the expensive rugs would get worn and trodden in.

Aurelio entered the kitchen, and when he spotted Tomas, a tired smile split across his face. "Well, you're a sight for sore eyes," he murmured as his gaze drank in Tomas's nude body. "To what do I owe this pleasure?"

Tomas smiled back as he ran a finger lightly over his cock, tip to base. "Oh, no doubt you'll think of something." He didn't miss the sudden shadow of fatigue that floated across Relio's face. Come to think of it, the man didn't look well at all.

Tomas stood up and walked over to his lover. "Are you okay? You look rather beat."

Relio huffed. "I have been feeling a little unwell this evening. If you don't mind, I will have a quick shower and get into bed."

Tomas nodded solemnly. "I will join you after your shower. I promise to leave you alone and not start any mind-blowing sex."

Aurelio reached out a warm hand and caressed Tomas's jawline. "You are difficult to resist, *tesoro*, especially naked like this. I am sorry to spoil your surprise." He shrugged elegant shoulders. "I think I need some sleep. It might be a stomach bug going around or something. I am sure in the morning I'll feel much better." He placed a brief kiss on Tomas's lips. "Let me go clean up. I'll be out soon."

Aurelio walked away, rubbing the back of his neck. Tomas watched him, feeling concerned. Aurelio was so strong and formidable and the thought of his man feeling ill and out of sorts didn't sit well with him. He'd wait until the morning to tell Relio that one of his people was missing. There was no point in worrying him with it tonight.

Perhaps he could give Aurelio as massage before he went to sleep, get rid of some obvious tension in his shoulders. Tomas went back into the lounge and tidied up, checking his emails in case there was anything from Tanvi. There was nothing, and she hadn't called either.

Tomas knew welfare checks could take a while to arrange, so he knew he needed to be patient. He responded to a few emails and then finally, he shut his laptop.

The apartment was quiet, no sounds of water. Tomas glanced down at his watch, taken aback by how late it was. One am. He'd got so caught up in his work he'd lost track of time.

He packed up his stuff and then quietly stole into the bedroom. There, on top of the covers, clad only in his silk night shorts, Aurelio lay fast asleep on his stomach. His dark hair framed his aquiline face and his proud roman nose. One arm was flung out to his side, while the other was hidden under the plumpness of his pillow.

Tomas took a moment to admire Relio's body, the strong back muscles, the long, elegant legs sprinkled with dark hair. Tomas bent over and placed a line of soft, butterfly kisses down Relio's spine, half hoping it would wake him up. Relio murmured, smiled and snuggled deeper into the bed. Tomas sighed and draped the cover over his man then climbed in beside him. He lay on his side watching Relio sleep for a while then as his own eyelids started to droop, Tomas settled into his bed and joined his lover in sleep.

Chapter 3

Clay rolled his neck, wincing at the ominous sounds of cracking bone and creaking cartilage.

"I heard that," Tate observed with amusement. "I thought I was the one with the dodgy neck?"

Clay scowled at his partner from across the dining room table. "You don't have the monopoly on crappy physiology. I swear since I turned forty, my body is falling apart." He regarded Tate gloomily. "At least I wasn't getting blown up last night. Are you sure you're okay? I'm still worried about that bruising on your back."

Tate shook his head. "I'm fine. Hurt like shit for a while but," he shrugged, "it's not like I'm not used to it."

Clay leaned back in his chair, fingers playing idly with the napkin at the side of his now empty plate. Hearing the news about the explosion last night had given him palpitations, as he'd imagined Tate lying in pieces somewhere. Hearing Tate's voice on the phone some bystander had kindly loaned him had been a relief of note.

I'm getting too old for this crap. Thank God he and Ellis came out of everything unharmed.

"Have you heard anything back yet from the fire department?" Tate shook his head. "I guess it's too soon for them to be making a judgment whether it was a natural event or arson." Clay scoffed, "We all know it was deliberate. There's no way that happened by accident. A critical witness being barbequed minutes before he's being picked up to give evidence goes beyond the bounds of accident. It also tells me we have a leak somewhere. Only a few people knew you and Ellis were going down there to pick him up."

Tate's eyes narrowed. "I hear you. I've asked Tomas to do some checking on everyone that knew about it. Perhaps he can come up with something."

"They've discovered two bodies, both have gone to the coroner," Clay said grimly. "I don't think there's much doubt one of them is Smokey."

They were silent for a minute as they contemplated what that could mean. Clay decided he wouldn't dwell on it. Tomas would find something if it was there and if not, well, then Clay would make another plan to discover who might have got Tate and Ellis killed. His team were good at ferreting out the truth, He had faith they'd find the leak.

He stood and cleared away their breakfast dishes, remnants of a full English, one of their Sunday treats, taking the plates and cutlery to the sink, rinsing them, then loading them in the dishwasher. When he turned around, Tate was right there behind them, smiling gently.

"I'm fine," he murmured, as his hands brushed Clay's cheek and his body pressed comfortingly against Clay's. "It takes a lot more than being blown up to get rid of me." He leaned in and laid a soft kiss on Clay's lips. "You more than anyone should know that."

Clay leaned his forehead against Tate's. "Yeah, but that's the problem," he joked weakly. "You *are* accident-prone."

Tate chuckled, a throaty sound that stirred Clay's soul. "I promise I'll try to stay out of trouble." He moved away, toward the table and collected the other breakfast debris. "Archie is being awfully quiet. What did you do with him, lock him in the bedroom by mistake?"

Their French bulldog puppy, while loved to bits by them both, was turning into quite a handful. The pup had chewed Clay's favourite loafers into pieces with only the leather sole remaining. Tate's treasured Iron Maiden tee-shirt had also been ripped to shreds. Archie was a chewer, about that, there was no doubt. And when the five-month-old pup went silent and wasn't scrounging breakfast titbits, it was time to worry.

Clay looked around. "Not that I know of. The bedroom door was open last I remember." A sense of apprehension flooded his body. "Shit. We're bad parents, aren't we? I should have realised he wasn't around begging for my bacon."

Tate sniggered. "No, that would be *me* begging for your meat."

Clay groaned. "That's awful. Really?" He called out. "Archie? Where are you, boy? Come on out where we can see you."

The silence heightened Clay's unease. Tate tried calling out to Archie to but still they heard nothing. They exchanged a worried glance then started for the bedroom.

"I swear," Tate said between gritted teeth, "if that little shit has destroyed another of my shirts, I will lose my rag. He'll get no more damn treats for a week. No, make that a month."

Clay sniggered. "Listen to us, threatening our canine. It's a pity we can't ground him or take away his computer privileges."

They both reached the bedroom and peered cautiously into the room. Tate heaved a sigh of relief when he saw his shirt still lying on the floor. "Well, my gear is still intact," he said with satisfaction.

Clay stared in horror at the unholy mess in Tate's corner of the room. "If you picked your stuff up and put it away as I've asked you to, you wouldn't have to worry," he griped. "We have a laundry basket, you know."

Tate ignored him as he backed out of the room and into the kitchen. "Archie? Come on, boy. I have a treat for you." Usually, at the word treat the pup would come running. This time there was no scamper of little paws on the tiled floor, no saliva drooling little imp smiling up at them with a toothy grin.

"I hope he's okay," Clay gnawed at his lip as they searched the other rooms. "What if he got out of the grounds?" Their big Victorian house had been puppy-proofed, but a determined dog could probably find a way out into the street. So far, Archie hadn't been interested in anything beyond the red brick walls, but you never knew.

A flash of apprehension crossed Tate's face. "Jesus, I hope he hasn't," he muttered. "God, I didn't know having a damn dog would give me grey hairs like this—" His voice broke off as he stared inside the palatial bathroom. "Oh, fuck me. That's why he's been so quiet."

Clay pushed past him to see what Tate was looking at. His jaw dropped and he could only stare in dismay at the havoc one small pup had wreaked.

Toilet paper rolls, a whole bag of them from the looks of it, lay scattered across the floor, tissue paper in chunks and shreds in long trails like rail tracks across the bathroom floor. In mayhem's midst, loo roll draped across his head, Archie sat, tail wagging proudly as if to say, "It attacked me, but I made it pay, oh yes I did. See me roar."

Clay couldn't stifle the urge to laugh. What a bloody mess, but a cuter sight he'd never seen.

"I thought you said you'd put the toilet rolls away safely out of his reach," Tate muttered, and from the sound of his voice he was struggling not to laugh. "I distinctly remember saying you would."

Clay looked at his lover shamefacedly. "I meant to, but I got distracted."

"And you tell me to put my stuff away," Tate teased. "So that means you play bad cop with him."

Clay heaved a sigh. "I guess that's only fair." He went into the bathroom and stood over the pup, whose tail was still wagging madly.

"Bad boy," Clay scolded. "This is not a good thing."

Archie regarded him with a serene expression. He didn't seem too fazed that Clay was unhappy. "You've been a naughty dog," Clay tried again, lips twitching as Archie moved and the toilet roll slid off his head. "Now I have to clean this mess up. Go outside and think about what you've done."

"Oh yeah," Tate remarked. "That's a bad cop there all right. I'd be shaking in my boots, Not."

Archie gave a short bark and scampered past them both, as his paws clattered down the hallway toward the kitchen. No doubt he thought he'd be rewarded for slaying the toilet paper villain.

"Well, I tried," Clay argued. "But did you see how bloody adorable he looked?" He set about picking up the paper strewn across the floor and dumped it all into the bath. He'd get a garbage bag when it was all picked up and take it out to the rubbish.

After a minute, Tate sighed and started to help. "We will need more loo roll," he suggested. "We can salvage what we can, but I'm not hopeful. I think he vanquished the beast."

They looked at each other and burst into laughter. This was one of Clay's favourite parts of having a relationship. The camaraderie and knowledge that your other half would always be there to help you clean up in life, no matter what it took.

***

When Tate's mobile rang a few hours later, Clay was sitting reading in his easy chair close to the fireplace. Logs crackled in the hearth and the flames reflected across the dimly lit walls. The living room was warm and toasty while outside the wind howled in the late November night. It had been bitterly cold the last few days and Clay was thinking of getting the electric blanket out for their bed.

In the corner, in his doggie bed, Archie snored as he slept, little limbs twitching no doubt with thoughts of chasing rabbits or perhaps even tearing up another pair of Clay's shoes. Clay smiled at the sight. The little puppy had become an integral part of their little family, and while he was often mischievous, he was obedient to a fault and quick to learn. His training was going along splendidly, and the days Tate and Clay spent out in the open field at the dog training facility nearby had become a treat for them all.

Tate picked up his phone from where he was stretched across the couch watching something on Sky Arts about street art. "Tomas. How are you doing?"

Clay glanced across the room, then went back to reading. He hoped nothing had happened between Tomas and Relio. Those two beat Clay and Tate at the "I love you, I hate you" game and their relationship was never a cert. At present, Clay understood everything was good with them so hopefully this wasn't a call that would refute that.

"I see. How long has she been missing?" Tate stood up and strode over to the hall table, pulling the drawer out to remove a writing pad and a pen. "Uh-huh. And you say the welfare check showed nothing out of place?" He wrote some words down on the pad as Clay stared on curiously.

"Okay. Does Aurelio know you've called us in on this one?" Tate waited then huffed. "Sure he does. Right, there's not much we can do tonight. We'll come by tomorrow, see you, look at her place if we can get access to it, and maybe ask a few questions to the other shopkeepers. Perhaps someone saw something." He broke off, listening intently. "That's fine, Tomas. We won't call the police yet. I agree, they're probably getting sick of the Alley issues by now, but Rick will understand." The loud, excited garble from the other side of the phone had Tate rolling his eyes. "I promise, drama llama. No getting the cops involved. Geesh, calm down, will you? See you tomorrow then. Eleven a.m."

He clicked off his phone and looked over at Clay. "A young woman has been missing for a few days and no one knows where she is. He's asked us to see if we can help."

Clay moved across the room and turned his backside to the fire, warming himself. "What do they think happened? Anyone got any ideas?"

Tate shook his head. "Not really, although she has an abusive boyfriend issue." He scowled. "Tosser apparently likes to hit women. Her name's Olivia, she's twenty-three, and she works with Tanvi at that chocolate shop in the alley. The one with the life-size vagina in the window. Olivia's been missing since Friday, and her not calling in is uncharacteristic."

Clay blinked and sat back down, his arse toasty. "And they've only called in someone now? Why so late? The first twenty-four hours are the most critical."

Tate shrugged. "Apparently Tanvi started getting worried on Saturday when Olivia didn't show up for work. She requested a welfare check last night, thinking maybe the boyfriend had done something to her. The cops went out there early hours of this morning and there's no one home. No signs of anything untoward, no signs of a struggle."

Clay rubbed his chin thoughtfully. "So we're meeting Tomas and Relio tomorrow at the club?"

"Yep. We can look at her flat, and do some recon with the neighbours, find out if they saw anything." Tate walked into the kitchen to make a fresh pot of coffee. Archie yawned widely, blinked a few times, and got out of his bed to follow Tate. "It could be she's gone away on holiday and forgot to tell anyone. Or got shitfaced somewhere and is sleeping it off. Tomas has already done the whole checking the morgue and hospital thing."

He chuckled as he handed Clay a cup. "He'll land himself in a heap of trouble if he keeps hacking government and civil sites as he does. That young man has no boundaries." Tate motioned to Archie. "Come on boy, you can sit with me." He patted the couch next to him and Archie wasted no time jumping up with a smug glance at Clay. He'd given up asking Tate not to encourage the dog on the furniture or the bed. It was a fight he seemed destined to lose.

"Ain't that the truth," Clay agreed as he sipped his coffee, humming in appreciation at the rich taste and aroma." He stifled a yawn. The heat from the fire had made him drowsy, and he glanced down at his watch. Eleven p.m. Perhaps he'd read a little more then call it a night.

Tate got comfortable with Archie on the couch, as the pup wriggled his little backside into position and once again cast a smug look in Clay's direction. Tate flicked the TV volume up, soon engrossed in a programme about parasites in the human body. Clay cringed at the thought of even watching that show. Who the hell wanted to know all about the things that lived in and on your body? It was as creepy as hell, but it seemed to satisfy Tate's need for the macabre and the ghoulish.

An hour later Clay finished his reading and stood up, stretching. "I'm off to bed." He leaned down and pressed a kiss to the top of Tate's head. He did the same to Archie who opened one eye blearily then went back to sleep. "See you both in a little while?"

Tate nodded, eyes still fixed in fascination on the screen. "I'll be up in a minute. I want to see how the doctor sorts this one out." He motioned to the TV with the remote. "That woman has some bug living in her eye."

Clay shuddered at the thought. He'd seen men blown to bits, gunshots, stabbings and even the occasional burn victim, but nothing got to him more than the thought something could grow inside his body and cause havoc.

"I don't know how you can watch those programmes before you go to bed," he muttered to Tate as he left the room. "They'd give me nightmares."

"Such a wuss," Tate teased. "It's nature, babe. Scarier than anything you or I could dream up."

Up in the bedroom, Clay had a shower, towelled dry and pulled on a pair of black briefs. He crawled into bed, put his head on the pillow, and was asleep in minutes.

***

Oh God, that feels so good. Clay thrust his hips up into the warmth of the mouth surrounding his dick and moaned softly when the pressure on his hard-on increased while teasing lips and a strong, wet tongue circled the tip.

This dream is realistic. It's been a while since I had one of these. I hope I stay asleep long enough to come.

He wanted to curse when that heated and clever mouth stopped what it was doing. *This is my fucking dream, and I don't want it to stop.*

"It's not a dream, baby," Clay faintly heard Tate murmur amusedly.

Once again, Clay's dick was engulfed and this time, Tate's fingers pulled on his balls, caressing, stroking and slid through the moisture around his aching cock, finding his sensitive hole. Clay groaned and finally opened his eyes. It was morning dark in the room, and somewhere below the covers, a figure moved, one finger slowly circling Clay's opening, teasing him by sliding in and out, making Clay want so much more.

His body tensed as Tate's mouth played him like he was devouring a lollipop, sucking and slurping. "T, I'm about to blow," he got out with a strangled gasp, the sly insistence of fingers now pressing inside Clay's arse too much to bear.

"That's the point, honey. I want to taste you. Gill my mouth," Tate murmured, around his mouth full of cock. "Maybe all you need is more encouragement."

The finger now deep in Clay's arse found the spot that promised heaven and rubbed it, and Clay erupted with a loud roar of satisfaction. "Jesus Christ..." he grunted as he shot his load into his fiancé's greedy mouth.

There was a low chuckle from under the duvet and Tate's tousled head appeared, lips swollen from his endeavours was still licking come from his the corner of his mouth. "Not Jesus, babe, but close enough."

Tate pushed the covers back behind him and straddled Clay as Tate's hand worked his own dick and his face creased in pleasure. "Love waking you up like this, then coming all over you. Love owning you." His hand worked faster. Clay watched in fascination as Tate's throat flushed pink, his eyes closing in orgasmic relief, his cock a deep plum colour and aching to let loose. There was something primal about this as if sex, passion and sheer animal need was the only thing they needed, gentrification and manners be damned.

Tate gave his own shout of pleasure as streams of thick, white come shot across Clay's chest and stomach, some even hitting his chin before Tate collapsed, gasping on top of Clay whose arms wrapped around his lover, stroking his flanks and heated backside. For a while, neither man spoke, content to be stuck together by combined fluids of semen and sweat, hearts beating in tandem as their breathing slowed and pulse rates decelerated.

Tate rolled off Clay and lay on his back. He glanced mischievously at his lover, idly tracing the mess on Clay's stomach with a finger. "Are you properly awake now? I thought it was about time I got you out of bed. It's nine am already."

"Jesus." Clay shot up, groping for his mobile. "Why the heck did you let me sleep so late? I have a conference call in fifteen minutes." He scrambled out of bed, hunting for his trousers and shirt. There was no way he'd have time for a shower before his Skype call, so he'd have to clean himself up as best he could and shower afterward.

Tate smirked. "I rather like the idea of you sitting all prim and proper there in front of your laptop knowing you have my come all over you."

Clay snorted and wiped himself cleaner with wet wipes. "Sorry, babe. I can't in all honesty sit and face Raymond to talk about industrial espionage feeling sticky and smelling like a man-slut. Your chest-beating alpha male shit will have to take a back seat." He dressed quickly, looking around the room. "Where's Arch? You didn't bring him to bed last night?"

Tate shook his head. "Nah. He was fast asleep in his bed downstairs, so I left him there. He knows where we are if he wants to go out."

"I'll give him a run in the garden before my call." Clay tried to comb his hair into order. He needed coffee stat, and that would be the next thing on his agenda after letting the pup out to perform his business. Their dog walker came by twice a day to let the pup out and take him for exercise while they were at work.

Clay left Tate lolling in bed and made his way down the curved staircase. Archie greeted him at the bottom, tail wagging and scuttled toward the back door. Clay grinned as he found the keys and opened it, watching the little muscly ball of fur with his powerful, short legs dash into the garden and stand there with a beatific look on his scrunched-up face. Archie hadn't yet learnt to cock his leg when he peed. Clay left him to his business and hurried into his study, powering up his laptop and starting Skype. It always seemed to take a little while to load.

While it did, he went into the kitchen and started the coffee machine. "Never let it be said men can't multi-task," he muttered as he poured coffee grinds and water into the machine. "I don't think I do too badly."

That done, he reached into the dishwasher to take out two cups—he may as well make Tate a cup too—and soon the kitchen was filled with the heavenly the aroma of freshly brewed coffee. That alone was usually guaranteed to get his lazy sod out of bed.

Not a bad start to my day, Clay mused as he carried the coffee upstairs.

I'm a lucky man.

Chapter 4

"What's on the cards first?" Clay asked as he and Tate strode down Fetish Alley, scarves wrapped around their throats and shivering despite their heavy jackets. An icy wind blew down the street, and frost sparkled on lamp posts and windowsills where the glass was steamy with condensation.

The road trip had been precarious, the bike needing careful handling on the icy streets. Tate had hung on for dear life as Clay manoeuvred the beast through traffic, slippery corners and a handful of idiotic car drivers who didn't give a fuck for bikers.

Tate pushed his hands deeper into his jacket pockets. He wore fingerless gloves—something that drove Clay crazy as he said he'd never see the point of them, he wanted his whole hand warmed, thank you very much—and a black beanie that extended over his ears.

"I said we'd meet Tomas first at the club, get the story out of him and what he's done so far to find his friend. Then we'll pop down to the shop and speak to Tanvi." He took his hands out of his pocket and blew warm air on them. "Christ, it's freezing. Have I told you how much I hate the cold?"

"Every time the temperature drops below 18 degrees," Clay remarked drily. "Maybe if you wore a pair of proper gloves, you wouldn't have to heat your fingers up."

Tate scowled. "I like these. Jax bought them for me." Tate stopped to peer into a shop window, a sign outside proclaiming it as "Lewd Foods." He chortled as he took stock of some items in the steamy window. "Look, they sell rimming sugar in many flavours. I can give myself a sweet treat next time I'm eating your arse."

"My arse is tasty enough without sugar," Clay retorted with a grin. "Maybe we need some of that Jamaican Jerk sauce lube for yours though. Hot and spicy, like you." Both men tittered and then looked around to see if anyone had heard them acting like teenagers.

"They have a load of rude sounding stuff in here," Tate said as cleared the window with his glove and stared inside with fascination. "Plopp chocolate, Cemen dip, pulled pork crisps. Maybe we should get Jax and Dare a hamper for Christmas."

Clay laughed. "I like that idea. Let's keep it in mind. We always struggle to find them something."

They continued walking, the street getting busier with every step. Fetish Alley was waking up. Soon, unveiling before a faint mist that had crept in from nowhere, Aurelio's club, Graffiato Animé, loomed before them. With Christmas only six weeks away, he had paid homage to the season by planting half a dozen small conifers in deep red urns outside the entrance. The urns were surrounded by white fairy lights, the door festooned with a giant wreath of pinecones, foliage and berries, adding a festive air to the place. All the external windows held window boxes filled with red and green flowers, and Tate had to admit that the club held a warm and welcoming festive appeal.

"It looks good," he acknowledged as they climbed the steps and he rang the bell. "I guess we need to think about whether we're doing anything with our place this year or not." His tone was teasing. He knew Clay loved Christmas, the hustle and bustle of it, the glitter and sparkle, and the smell of mulled wine and warm gingerbread. Tate teased him about it unmercifully, calling him a magpie for all things shiny.

Clay stared at him in horror. "Of course we are. Maybe not a tree and baubles, but a wreath or two, and a few ornaments scattered around, perhaps some fresh vines strung up along the stair balustrade. Jax and Dare will come over for lunch. Aurelio and Tomas too, perhaps."

Tate grinned. "Okay, keep your hair on."

It wasn't the religious essence of the season that appealed to Clay but the camaraderie and spirit of a chill and snowy December. Tate admitted there was something about being home in front of a roaring fire, surrounded by people you love and a good glass of wine or whisky, that made his inner child hum in delight too.

The door opened, and Cleaver stood there, his huge frame blocking the door. "Morning, gents," he boomed as he motioned them in. "The youngster said you were coming. Nice to see you both again, albeit under sad circumstances."

"Sad?" Tate's heart beat faster. "Have they found her?" *God, please don't tell me there's another Fetish Alley body.*

Cleaver shook his head as he took their jackets and adeptly made them disappear into a huge closet under the stairs. "No, sorry, I meant, it's sad that she's missing, you know?"

"Oh." Tate sighed with relief, as did Clay. "Well, we hope to find her."

"I know if anyone can, you two will." Cleaver motioned them into the study. "Relio and Tomas are waiting in here."

Clay walked ahead, Tate following. The study door clicked shut behind them. Relio sat behind his desk, in conversation on his mobile with someone in rapid-fire Italian. Tomas was on the couch, a computer on his lap, clicking madly at his keyboard. He looked up as they entered, a huge grin flooding across his face.

"Hey, guys." He laid his laptop down and bounded to his feet. He came over and shook first Clay's then Tate's hand. "It's great to see you both again. Have a seat." Tomas picked up his computer and set it upon the desk. "I'm sure Relio will arrange some refreshments soon."

Tate sat down on the couch and Clay followed suit. "Looks as if you have it all sussed," Tate said slyly. "Have you been staying here long then? How's your flat in Knightsbridge?"

Tomas waved a hand. "Pfft. I spend so little time there nowadays. I seem to be here most of the time. Relio needs looking after." He winked at Tate. "The man can be a little uptight and I am trying hard to get him to relax."

"You'll get no arguments from me," Tate murmured. "I take it things are going okay between you now then?"

I can't even count the number of times you two have been off and on since you started.

Tomas shrugged. "I think. He is my Daddy Bear, and I am his cub." Tomas's eyes twinkled as Clay's jaw dropped. "Make of that what you will."

"Tomas." Aurelio's voice was quiet but commanding. Clay glanced across at his friend as he set down his phone and cast a stern glance at Tomas. "I do not think Tate and Clay wish to know the intimate details of our relationship. We discussed this."

"Oh please, carry on," Tate encouraged and grinned as Clay groaned loudly. I'm going to milk this as much as I can. "I for one would love to hear the juicy details about what sounds like a charming woodsy fairy tale. Tell me, Cub, does Daddy Bear enjoy your honey?"

"God, T," Clay spluttered between laughs. "Was that necessary?"

Tomas sidled over to Aurelio and slipped into his lap. "Did I step over the line? Will you punish me later?" His fingers played softly across Aurelio's chin, his hand moving down over Aurelio's throat, where his pulse beat rapidly.

Aurelio caught Tomas's hand as he cast a frosty glance at Tate who stared back, unfazed. A lesser man would have slunk out of the room with his tail between his legs.

"Perhaps." Aurelio snapped but his eyes sparkled with amusement. "Then again, perhaps there will be no punishment and I will send you to bed to think about what you have done. Now behave, please. We have business to discuss."

Tomas pouted. "Fine. I'll be good." He uncurled his lithe form from Aurelio's lap and picked up his laptop, plonking himself down into the one and only easy chair, legs crossed beneath him. "Let's get started then." He looked up. "Where would you like to begin?"

Tate pursed his lips. "I have some questions. I'll start. You answer. Firstly, tell us about Olivia. Where she works, what she does, who her friends are. We need background info."

Tomas took a deep breath. "Olivia works at Chocerotica as a sales assistant. She works part-time, and some Saturdays. I have become something of a friend because she shares my passion for jigsaw puzzles. We swap our favourites." He made a sad moue. "She doesn't have a lot of friends because of that arsehole of a boyfriend. He frightens people."

Tate hadn't thought someone as hyperactive as Tomas would have the patience to do something like a jigsaw puzzle. "And how long has she been missing?"

"Since she did not turn up for work on Friday. Tanvi thought perhaps she was sick. She tried to call her but there was no reply. Then on Saturday, there was no communication from her either. On Sunday, as you know, Tanvi requested a welfare check, and the police found nothing. No signs of a struggle."

"Was her handbag and her phone still in her flat?" Clay leaned forward, face set. "Any pets that weren't fed, anything out of the norm?"

Tomas shook his head. "She has no pets. Her phone and bag are missing but her phone must be turned off because I cannot trace her." He scowled. "The police who did the welfare check looked around."

"Olivia is a lovely young lady," Aurelio added, his expression worried. "It is most unlike her to cause people concern like this. Tanvi is beside herself." He rang a little bell on his desk. Tate assumed it was to summon someone. It was all very "upstairs-downstairs."

"Sometimes people get into relationships they feel they can't get out of," Tate said. "Believe me, I know." He was interrupted by the door opening as Cleaver posted his massive bulk in the doorway.

Aurelio smiled at him. "Cleaver, thank you. Please ask Siobhan or Greg to send the lunch trays through. I think our guests must be hungry and thirsty."

Cleaver nodded, his dreads swinging around his face. "Sure, boss. No problem." He disappeared quicker than Tate thought a man of his size could move.

"I have put the word out in the alley for any information. We've also had some posters printed and they are being put up all over the place." Tomas flicked a glance at Tate. "Your friends Josiah and his crew were happy to help. They're good people."

"The alley is pulling together to do its bit," Aurelio muttered. "Olivia is one of our own. I'd expect nothing less." There was no arrogance in Aurelio's tone, only a matter-of-factness that the people he was crowned king of would do everything in their power to do what he asked.

Aurelio had earned the trust of all the alley people and no one would ever protect them and look after them like he would and did.

"So... she's been gone a few days, nothing untoward in the flat, bag and phone gone, and no one has a clue where she might be," Clay mused. "Does she have a family she might have gone to?"

Tomas shook his head vehemently. "No, her parents are dead. She was an only child. Her aunt lives in South America somewhere and she's the only relative Livvy had."

"I take it you checked hospitals and morgues?" Tate confirmed and sighed resignedly as Tomas gave him a scathing glance.

"Of course," Tomas muttered. "That was the first thing I did. I have alerts set up if anything new comes in, but thank God so far there has been nothing reported."

The room went silent. Tate supposed the fact nothing had been reported was a blessing, but it also meant that Olivia was out there somewhere, possibly hurt, or worse, dead, and no one knew where.

"We need to speak to Tanvi and the boyfriend." Tate stood and paced around the room. "The thing about missing people is finding out as much info as we can about them and retracing their steps to the minute they disappeared, if we can." He turned to Tomas. "I imagine you checked the CCTV footage? Did you find anything?"

Tomas nodded. "I have the last image of Libby walking down Shetland Street, away from the cinema where she left her boyfriend. The timestamp was seven eleven pm. There's nothing else since." He picked up a sheet of paper from the desk. "I downloaded one of her Facebook pictures and printed it out. That's what the guys are using to post around the area. Here." He shoved the paper at Tate who took it. A picture of a young, pretty, smiling young woman with strawberry blonde hair and bangs stared out at them.

"We'll double-check what's down Shetland Street and see if anyone in the area saw her." Clay stood up and crouched down next to Tomas who looked down at him, eyes stormy. "Tomas, you know we will not be able to leave the police out of this. They will need to be involved soon."

Tomas grew agitated. "You know how I feel about the cops. They are useless. And corrupt."

"*Tesoro*, you had a problem with one or two policemen back in your country. This is England. It will not be the same." Aurelio looked at Tomas with empathy. "I understand your reticence, but Clay is right. We won't be able to keep this a secret. It must be reported soon. A young woman's life is at stake."

"Rick will do the right thing," Tate murmured. "You trust me, don't you?" Tomas nodded. "Well, trust Rick too. He's family. He'll try to help any way he can. We will need access to resources only the police have."

Tomas didn't look convinced, merely snorted in disdain and bit down on his bottom lip as he folded his arms across his chest. He didn't argue anymore though, and for that Tate was thankful. He wondered though what trouble Tomas had got into in his home country that gave him such a hatred of law enforcement.

A young woman knocked on the half-open door and entered bearing a tray of sandwiches and snacks. Behind her, Cleaver carried a tray of coffee. They set the refreshments down on the low coffee table in one corner of the study then left as silently as they'd entered.

While Tate busied himself getting food and drink for them both, he saw Clay going over the notes he'd jotted down. "Here you go." Tate handed Clay a small plate loaded with carbs and other high-calorie treats. "I put your coffee beside you."

Clay nodded his thanks and bit into what looked like a chicken mayo sandwich quarter. "Once we're done here, we'll go talk to Tanvi."

Tate pushed a whole quarter sandwich into his mouth and spoke around it. "Uh-huh. The more info we can gather, the better."

It was close to half an hour later when Clay and Tate left the club to visit Tanvi after calling ahead to make sure she was there. The shop-owner sounded worried and Tate hoped that she'd be able to shed further light on Olivia's potential whereabouts.

Tanvi greeted them with a strained smile and gestured to the pair to join her in the open atrium at the back of the store. Tate loved the glass conservatory, filled with green plants and orchids which seemed to serve as Tanvi's workspace when she wasn't in the store's front.

"Please, have a seat. Push the cats off the couch and don't let them bother you." She shooed one cat away as Tate picked up another and plopped it down onto the floor. Once they'd sat down, she stared over at them with some apprehension.

"I don't know whether I'm being stupid worrying about Olivia, but I can't help feeling something is wrong. I'm not usually fanciful, but even Eleanor has said my aura is muddy. She told me worry will do that." Her dark eyes bore into me with trepidation. "Olivia has always been very reliable and her relationship with that awful boyfriend of hers has always been a concern." She hesitated. "I had to file a missing person's report on her with the police. I had no choice. Anything could have happened, especially with Allan in the picture."

Tate shrugged. "It's probably the best thing to do. And don't worry, we will visit this Allan too. He sounds like a nasty bit of work and if he had anything to do with this, you can bet we'll sort him out. You say you last saw Olivia on Wednesday because she had Thursday off?"

Tanvi nodded. "Yes, that's right."

Clay consulted his notebook. "Did she have any friends we can talk to, perhaps see if they can shed any light on her disappearance? We already have her boyfriend down as someone to speak with but there must be others." He reached down and stroked a ginger tabby winding itself in and out of his legs. Tate smiled at the sight.

It'll give Archie something different to sniff later when we get home.

Tanvi snorted loudly. "That man of hers is a waste of space and a bully. He verbally abused her all the time, and I know for a fact he's hit her. She wouldn't see sense when Tomas and I told her to give him the boot." She stopped, her brow furrowed in thought. "Olivia is not very sociable. She's shy and finds it hard to make friends. The only person I've really seen her interact with in the shop is Tomas, because who can resist him," she smiled fondly." Also, a young man who works for a competitor close to the high street." She gave an unladylike snort. "That place isn't really a competitor, only another boring commercial chocolate kitchen making the usual stuff. Not like my kitchen. We're a little more creative in our designs."

Tate bit back a smile at the disdain in Tanvi's voice. "Who is this young man?"

"His name is Joshua. He's a bit of an introvert but he and Olivia seem to get on well enough." She frowned. "They aren't bosom buddies, but I suppose it might be worth having a chat with him. There's also a young lady called Charlotte whom Olivia is friendly with who comes into the shop regularly. She works in Lewd Foods behind the counter."

Clay nodded. "What's the name of the place he works at? And we'll pop into Lewd Foods and speak to Charlotte.

Tanvi sniffed. "Joshua works at Chocolate Heaven. *Really* original name."

Tate chuckled at Tanvi's scorn. "Okay. We'll pop over there and have a chat with him as well. As you say, we need to follow up every lead we can get."

He and Clay took a quick look in Olivia's work locker. A pink cashmere sweater, hair scrunchies, two leaflets for Concerts in the Park, already done and dusted, and an empty water bottle gave no clue where she might be. After a fruitless search, they headed over to visit Olivia's boyfriend, Allan.

Chapter 5

The tube was packed, and Clay held onto the overhead rail for dear life as the train hurtled around yet another corner. There'd been no point taking the bike out again when the next interviewee worked at a shop only a few stops away. Allan Smith worked at a branch of an electronics store near Embankment. Clay's mobile rang as they wobbled around yet another corner and he swore under his breath.

"Jesus, why does my phone always ring at the worst times?" Clay hated answering his phone on the tube. No one needed to know his business.

Tate nudged him, hazel eyes sparkling in amusement. "Like when we're in the middle of sex?" A faint bead of moisture clung to his cheek, as the air in the carriage filled with humans and sweaty odours had grown warmer.

Clay swore again and reached up with one gloved hand to brush the sweat off Tate's face. "Exactly like that." He ignored the scandalised glance of the man next to them, who moved away as much as he could in the crowded interior. "Whoever rang will have to wait until we get off this god-forsaken train."

As he said that, their station was announced, and Clay waited eagerly for the doors to open. Once they did, he was one of the first out onto the platform waiting for Tate, who'd got blocked behind an old lady and her walking cane. Clay took out his phone while he waited and smiled when he saw from whom the call had been.

"Jax called," Clay announced as Tate ambled up to his side. "I'll call him when we get to the coffee bar."

"We're having coffee again?" Tate murmured as they joined the throng of people trying to get out. "Didn't we already do that this morning?"

Clay stared at him in mock horror. "There's always time for coffee. Haven't I taught you anything?" They finally made it onto the escalator and started the slow crawl up toward daylight and coffee.

"You've taught me a lot," Tate quipped slyly. "I seem to remember once you showed me how to blow—"

Clay reached down and slapped one hand over Tate's mouth. "Not here," he hissed. "Keep your salacious remarks to yourself."

Tate blinked innocently. "What's the problem? I was going to say blow up the air bed without a pump. Remember, we had to use Jax's hairdryer?" He smirked. "Not everything is about you, sweetheart."

Clay turned back, refusing to show Tate he was laughing. God, how did he mat up with this man? But he knew why. Their relationship had been destined from day one. Clay had always felt that. No matter what they'd been through in the past, together was where they belonged and there was nothing he wouldn't do for Tate.

They reached the top of the escalator and stepped off, forging their way through the masses to the exterior. Once outside, Clay headed for the store he knew was on the next corner. "I'll give Jax a call later," he said. "We'll forgo the coffee and get this interview over. It's getting close to home time for commuters and I'd rather be on our way before the rush hour starts."

Tate whistled as he walked beside Clay, the epitome of casual yet tarnished elegance in his black jeans, grey button-up shirt, unbuttoned across his chest to show a hint of dark chest hair, and the silver chain around his neck.

God, he's fucking sexy. And all mine. Clay's groin tingled at the thought of pushing Tate face-first against the alley wall they'd passed, reaching around to unzip him, and take Tate's cock in his hand. Clay would thrust against Tate's sexy backside and get himself off while he drove Tate—

"You okay there? You look a little weird." Tate's question brought Clay back from his fantasies. Clay coughed and tried to look as if he hadn't been thinking about his ravishing his fiancé in public against an alley wall. His cock strained at the front of his chinos and he winced at the tightness.

"Yeah, I'm good," he said, voice husky. "Taking in the atmosphere, you know?"

Tate grinned, and Clay's traitorous dick gave another little lurch in his pants. *Christ, I'm like a horny teenager! What the hell is wrong with me?*

"That hottie you mean?" Tate gestured over to where a mime stood on an upturned box, standing stock still, and staring at the crown intensely. He was well-built and rather attractive, shirtless, and covered in silver paint. He carried a huge mock machine gun and resembled a soldier from some dystopian online game. Now and then, he'd make a robotic move and the gun would come up and point out into the watching crowd.

Clay nodded. "He looks convincing. I don't know how he stands there for hours without moving."

Tate shrugged. "Practice and patience." He flashed that grin again. "One, I'm good at, the other, not so much." His gaze grew heated. "And may I say, I think we might practise some other skills when we get home tonight. You're looking rather hot in that waistcoat. I think I'd like to take it off. Slowly."

Clay got out a strangled "Oh, really?" before Tate winked and sped ahead, still whistling. Clay cursed silently, willing his dick down and then strode after his lover. He glimpsed himself in a shop window and preened a little.

Much to his own surprise, Clay found he'd been happy to lose the formal business suits since moving their office to home. Instead, he now opted for dark chinos, a long-sleeved shirt and often, his favourite charcoal vintage waistcoat.

One had to have some class to one's outfit. Clay knew he could be a little pedantic about how he presented himself, but some things couldn't be compromised.

They reached the electronics shop and stepped inside to frigid air.

"Christ, it's like a freezer in here," Tate grumbled. "Way to make customers feel comfortable." He ambled over to the customer services desk as Clay looked around. He heard Tate flirting with the young woman and gave a wry smile. His fiancé could charm anyone out of their pants when he wanted to.

Tate came back and jerked a thumb over his shoulder. "Young Smith is in the back, bringing out a TV for a customer. The sales lady says she'll let him know we're here. She said it all swooningly, so I'm taking it she fancies him." His face darkened. "I bet if she knew he abuses his girlfriend she wouldn't feel that way." He turned and began browsing through the tablets displayed on the shelf.

Clay leaned against a pillar and crossed his arms as he waited. His phone vibrated in his pocket again and he pulled it out. Jax again. What was so urgent he'd keep calling? Clay felt a sense of misgiving as he answered.

"Jax? Sorry about earlier, I was on the tube."

"Hey, Clayzilla. No problem. It's not that desperate." Jax sounded tired and Clay's protective instincts ignited.

"You okay, baby bird? You sound down." Their pet names were still as endearing as they'd been when Tate had set them up when Jax had moved in with them all those years ago. They'd been emergency call signs in case anything bad had happened.

Tate stopped browsing an aisle away and turned to face Clay, brow furrowed. "He okay?" Tate mouthed.

God, his man had ears like a bat. Clay shrugged. "About to find out," he mouthed back.

Jax sighed. "I knew running a halfway house for kids would be one helluva journey but honestly, I never expected some things Dare and I have had to deal with. Sometimes, it gets me down, you know?"

"Jax, if anyone can do this, it's you. I take it things have been rough?" Clay juggled his phone so Tate could hear Jax too.

"You could say that. One of my kids killed herself last night." The pain in Jax's voice was raw and Clay's heart ached for hearing the pain in it. Jax had a birthday last month, and this was a crappy thing to happen even to a young man who'd lived a lifetime in his twenty-two years and understood the harsh life of the streets and foster care.

"Christ," he got out around the lump in his throat. He glanced at Tate, whose face had paled. "I'm so sorry. That's dreadful. Do you need us to come over later?"

There was silence, then, "Yeah, could you?" Jax's voice was strangled, sounding on the verge of holding back tears. "Dare is here with me now, but it would help a lot if you two were around for a bit if that's okay."

"We'll come over," Tate promised. "We'll swing by yours this evening and bring dinner. Tell that boyfriend of yours not to bother cooking."

"I will. He's not feeling good about all this either. We're both out of sorts." Jax sounded bewildered. "I mean, we had no idea that Sarah would do this. What does that say about me and my stupid psychology degree if I couldn't even figure that out?" His voice cracked and in the background, they heard Dare's gruff tone telling Jax it wasn't his fault.

"Listen to Dare, Jax." Clay wished he could find the magic words to make Jax feel better. "Don't get into that trap of blaming yourself. Believe me, Tate and I have both been there, and it's a road to nowhere. People do things of their own choosing. As much as we'd like to, we can't control their actions, and we can't save everyone."

Jax sniffed. "Yeah, yeah. I understand that, it's…" He huffed, "Look, I'll see you later, yeah, and we'll talk then. Sounds like you guys are shopping or something."

"Talking to acquaintances of a missing woman," Tate said and motioned toward a muscled younger man in a slim fit shirt approaching them. "So we'll be there later. Keep your game face on, champ. You can do this."

Jax mumbled something, and the phone went dead. Clay put his mobile back in his pocket, feeling useless to provide comfort. Put that aside for later and focus on the job, he counselled himself. He smiled at the man standing in front of them, who was thickset, with a gym body and close-cropped hair, and sported a trendy patch of stubble.

"Lacey said you wanted to see me about something?" Allan frowned. "What can I help you with?"

"We want to talk to you about your missing girlfriend," Clay said, and Allan's face darkened. "We thought you could help us with our enquiries."

"Are you the Old Bill?" Allan's face twisted in distaste. "Olivia isn't missing. She's fucking gone off with another bloke and is too scared to tell me."

"I guess she'd have reason to be scared," Tate said bitingly. "Given what we know of your relationship." He gestured to Allan's hands. "We understand you're a little free with those."

Allan's face flushed. "My relationship with my girlfriend is none of your fucking business. Now if you excuse me, I'm busy at work." He turned to go.

Clay reached out and pulled him back. "Not so fast. If you like, I can call my friend the actual cop and ask him to send a uniformed policeman to take you down to the station. Imagine how good that would look in front of your boss and colleagues. At least talking to us right here, we could be anyone, and no one would be the wiser."

Allan hesitated then sneered. "Fine. Ask your questions."

Ten minutes later, they had answers but none that he thought would help. He'd left her on Thursday evening around seven pm to walk home after the film. She'd said she wasn't feeling well. He'd been more than happy to let her go because according to him, his mates had invited him on a pub crawl. He'd gone off for a pint or two with his friends, and not seen her since. His messages the next day asking where she was hadn't been looked at. His phone calls had led to many voice mails, and his visit to her flat had garnered no response. He was quick to tell them he didn't have a key.

Allan Smith was an unpleasant individual, a bully and a bit of a jackass, but Clay's gut told him the boyfriend had anything to do with Olivia's disappearance. Judging from the frustration on Tate's face, he didn't think so either.

"If you find her, tell her we're over," Allan called out as they left. "I don't need to chase after a bit of skirt. There's plenty more where she came from."

"Such a fucking charmer," Tate muttered as they left the shop, and walked back down to the tube station. "I'd like to have a moment or two alone with him in a back alley, let him know what it feels like to be bullied."

Clay agreed. "I hate to say it, but I think we will have to get access to her flat, see if we can find anything the police may have missed on their welfare call," he muttered. "Maybe you could give Rick a call, see if he can spare anyone to let us in? We'll have to give him an update. Share what we've got."

Tate sighed. "Yeah, I'll do that. I'm not getting a good feeling about this one, Clay. A young woman disappears like this, without a history of it, I don't think it bodes well." His jaw tightened. "She's only a few years older than Jax, for God's sake."

And if Jax suddenly disappeared—well, Clay knew he and Tate would move heaven and earth to find him and damn the consequences. Speaking of Jax…

"Jax sounds cut up," Clay murmured as he and Tate walked back to the station. "I wish I could tell him everything would be okay, but we know that would be a lie. That boy feels deeply, and the things he's facing now will hurt him badly."

Tate's eyes shadowed. "I know," he said. "It breaks my heart he has to go through this. He'll see it as a personal failure even if you tell him a hundred times there's no guarantee on human behaviour. People do what they have to do." He huffed, "He's chosen a tough occupation, but he'll get over it. He's stronger than he thinks."

The journey to Fetish Alley to meet with Charlotte took about half an hour and was a disappointing visit. The young lady, bouncy and bubbly with a head of ginger curls, could offer no insight into Olivia's disappearance. They didn't hang out together after work, she explained, and the only time they chatted was in Chocerotica itself. Charlotte was coy about explaining her girlfriend really enjoyed some chocolate goodies available and they should try out the delectable chocolate body paint.

Clay knew *exactly* what she meant, having some already secreted away at home. Hmmm, he thought. Perhaps tonight might be the night to try it out.

***

Later that evening, when Jax opened the front door to his and Dare's red brick home in Swiss Cottage, Clay could see the toll the recent tragedy had taken on him. Jax was paler than usual, his pitted silvery facial scars more evident. He stared at them from milky blue eyes, surrounded by dark shadows, and mussed, slightly greasy blond hair.

"Hey, guys," he said wearily. "Thanks for coming over." He swallowed, looking close to tears. Dare hovered behind him, concern etched on his features, looking ready to move forward at a second's notice should his boyfriend need him. He acknowledged Clay and Tate with a solemn nod.

Clay got to Jax first, reaching out and drawing him in for a bear hug. "Of course," he said gently. "Where else would we be?"

Jax's arms wrapped around Clay's waist and his body shook with muffled sobs. Tate swore and sandwiched Jax in between the two of them, hugging Jax from behind. He handed the bags of Chinese food they'd bought on their way over to Dare, who took it with a strained smile.

"Get it all out," Tate said gruffly. "It's a shitty thing to happen and we'll talk about it in a minute, but for now, you stay here with us and let loose. We've got you."

Clay looked up and met Tate's eyes, which reflected the same pain. Tate knew first-hand about the loss of a young person to their own devices. Clay would never forget how broken up he'd been when a young girl called Lily had killed herself and Tate had been the one to find her.

They gave each other a rueful nod of understanding and went back to coddling the sobbing man in their arms. Clay's throat closed up. God, he thought, so this is what being a parent feels like. Unable to take away your children's pain, having to see them go through something they never should have experienced. He didn't have a clue how parents dealt with this from the start. He'd been a mess dealing with a Jax who'd been eighteen years old when he came to live with them.

Dare's face was pinched as he watched, letting Jax have his comfort with the two men he thought of as not only friends, but family.

When Jax's body stopped shuddering, he gently drew himself free of their embrace. Clay stepped back, and Tate did the same. Jax sniffed, eyes red and swollen but looking a little less stressed than before. Dare stepped forward and silently pressed a tissue into Jax's hand.

Jax gave a watery smile. "Thanks, babe. I think I might need another, though. My nose is all blocked." Clay and Tate turned away tactfully as Jax cleaned himself up and gave his nose a hearty blow.

"Go on into the living room," Dare said as he went into the kitchen. "I'll put some coffee on and bring it in. I'll pop the food on the table so you can all help yourselves when I bring the plates in."

Soon settled in the small, but cosy lounge, sipping their drinks, and nibbling at their food, Tate looked over at Jax, who was curled on the couch's corner next to Dare. Their shoulders touched, Dare's hand placed protectively on Jax's thigh.

"So tell us about what happened," Tate said. "As much as you feel comfortable sharing."

Jax took a deep breath and his left hand reached out to clutch convulsively at Dare's large hand. "Her name was Sarah. She was sixteen." He hiccupped a sigh. "Leon had been counselling her, and with her permission, I'd been sitting in on the sessions."

Jax had achieved his A levels in Psychology and was now studying further to become a counsellor. It was a long, hard slog, and while he and Dare owned the homeless shelter named Reach Out, Jax could not formally practice. Leon Davidson was the fully qualified and experienced manager of the centre, allowing Jax to gain on-the-job experience while studying part-time for his diploma.

"She seemed okay. She'd had a hard life. Her folks abandoned her when she was twelve and she lived on the streets for a long time." Jax looked down at his and Dare's conjoined hands, his gaze distant. "I can't tell you much, but what she went through wasn't pretty. Both Leon and I thought we were getting through to her but then..." His voice trailed off. "I got a hysterical call from one of her friends telling me Sarah had jumped off a bridge onto the carriageway. That suicide bridge in Islington. I forget the name."

"Jesus." Tate looked shaken. "Was anyone else hurt?"

Jax shook his head. "She left a note, saying she'd been careful not to hurt anyone else because that would be selfish. It was around three a.m. and the road was quiet."

The room went silent, no doubt everyone thinking about an emotional teenager all alone in her quest to die, yet still compassionate enough to be considerate of her fellow human beings.

Clay cleared his throat. "I know which bridge that is. It's the Archway Bridge. It's been notorious for suicides to the point the council will be putting in anti-suicide measures next year if it all passes planning." He puffed out his cheeks and blew out a soft breath of air. "Doesn't help right now though."

"Did she say anything else in her note?" Tate asked. "Give you any idea what drove her to that final step?"

Jax winced and looked over at Dare, who squeezed his hand comfortingly. "She thanked me and Leon for trying to help her," Jax whispered, his eyes shining. "She said we shouldn't blame ourselves for what she did, and that we'd been good friends to her. That she was tired of the struggle and saw death as the only answer." His hands fidgeted in agitation and Dare reached out and stayed them. "How can we get to such a place that a sweet sixteen-year-old kid thinks the only answer to her problems is to die?" A single tear fell from his left eye and Dare swept it away gently.

"Baby, the world is a mixed-up place," he murmured, eyes filled with pain. "And yeah, it sucks. You've got such a big heart, I can only imagine how much this hurts."

"Dare's right," Tate agreed. "You tried to do your best, but ultimately what Sarah did was her choice." His face was haunted. "Remember Lily, Jax? I thought I'd got through to her too. But it wasn't to be, and that's something we have no control over."

Jax nodded. "I remember you being a basket case for a while after it happened." He jerked a thumb toward Clay. "And you had the big guy there to help you through it. Like I've got my big lug here." He cast an affectionate glance at Dare who frowned.

"Big lug? I'm not sure if I'm supposed to be flattered or insulted." Dare's dark eyes warmed as Jax gave a little chuckle. "But if it cheers you up, then you can call me anything you like."

The rest of the evening, while a little less merry than usual, they'd achieved a level of comfort and it relieved Clay to see Jax laughing at something Tate had said. Clay knew it would take time for Jax's sense of helplessness for preventing the tragedy to fade, but it would.

All Jax needed was love and support, and between him, Tate and Dare, Jax had no shortage of it.

They left the couple around eleven pm and made their way home. Archie was thrilled to see them, darting about and looking longingly at the back garden. Clay fussed over him then turned to Tate. "You go upstairs. I'll sort out the pup and be in up in a moment."

Tate nodded with a smirk. "Don't be too long." He dashed up the stairs two at a time. Clay let Archie out for a pee and sniff around the garden and let him roam for a few minutes. When Archie came back in, he sauntered straight over to his basket and lay down with a grunt.

Clay ruffled his head as he walked past. "Night, Arch. See you in the morning."

When he got into the bedroom, it was dimmed, the only light on the lamp at the side of Clay's bed. He put his watch down on the side table. He was surprised Tate wasn't already under the covers. He must be in the bathroom, he thought. From underneath the closed door, a sliver of light shone. Clay shed his clothes, tossing them into the corner to put away tomorrow. As he snuggled under the duvet, the bathroom door opened. Outlined against the door, a naked Tate made a tantalising sight.

Clay crooked a finger, motioning him over. "Come on over here, babe. The bed is cold."

Tate sauntered into the room, his eyes gleaming. "Not for long. I have a treat for you." He loped over to Clay's side of the bed, his cock at a mouth-wateringly delectable angle for Clay to take into his mouth.

Clay cocked an eyebrow. "Is this a hint? Do you want a blow job? Happy to oblige."

Tate grinned and reached down to the bedside table to pluck something from the drawer. "First, you need to smear this all over me. Then I need you to lick it all off."

Clay peered at the label on the item in Tate's hand and looked up at him in fond exasperation. "How the hell did you find this? I hid it in my underwear drawer because God knows that's not a place you usually go." It was Clay's secret can of Belgian Body chocolate which had a small brush attached to the lid.

You spoilt my surprise, you sneaky bastard.

Tate smirked. "Babe, I know all your secret hiding places. I ran out of boxers, so I looked to borrow a pair of yours. And lo-and-behold, this is what I found." He wiggled the tin enticingly. "Now, hold on to your bollocks because this will get messy."

He walked over to the chest at the bottom of their bed where some spare bedsheets were stored and opened it. He drew out a spare sheet and threw it over at Clay. "Let's pop this on the bed then we can get as fucking down and dirty as we like."

Clay wasted no time and soon the sheet was down, his lover spread invitingly on the bed, hard cock pointed up and looking as if it needed a coat of chocolate. Tate's hard and muscled body was a delight to ogle and Clay anticipated covering it in the chocolate he now held, then licking it off and rolling around on the sheet body to body to see how much of the sticky sweet they could share.

"Cover me in chocolate, baby," Tate teased throatily. "And make sure every bit is cleaned off."

Clay wasn't sure whether he could use his mouth to do as commanded but he gave it his best shot. Soon he had a writhing, panting hot mess of a man squirming beneath him as Clay devoured his arse, his cock, the inside of his thighs and the hardened nipples that were so delightfully responsive to his probing tongue and sucking lips.

Tate tasted decadent, the chocolate covering his body filling Clay's mouth with sweetness with a hint of Tate's tang.

"Jesus, "Tate panted as he lay face down on the bed while Clay tried to reach a stubborn bit of chocolate between Tate's arse cheeks. "I will blow my load if you keep doing that. I want you inside me, so think carefully about where that fucking tongue of yours goes next...ahh, you bastard."

Clay delivered one last tonguing to Tate's crease then lifted his head and crawled up the bed to kneel beside Tate's sticky, heated, wriggling body. "Lie on your side, sweetheart, let me fuck you this way. I won't last much longer either. Christ, you are so hot when you're needy."

Tate turned onto his side and Clay positioned himself behind, his cock primed for entrance into Tate's hot, tight hole. "Going in," he murmured as he pushed slowly inside, shuddering in pleasure at the feel of his eager cock filling Tate's channel. Clay couldn't help himself, he started thrusting, seating himself deeper and deeper inside. Tate gripped Clay's head and pushed his hips back fiercely, desperately seeking Clay's mouth as he did. Their wet-tongued kisses tasted of chocolate and sweat, of masculine essences and the flavour of heavy passion.

Both men gasped each other's name as they came, Tate fisting his own cock as he emptied himself, Clay orgasming inside Tate, filling him with his come, and no doubt chocolate too. It had gone everywhere and Clay winced as he turned to lie flat on his back, his chest heaving. He was covered in sticky chocolate and semen.

"You're right," he slurred. "This was messy."

Tate chuckled tiredly as he turned to face Clay. "That's why they make washing machines." He wiped sweat out of eyes. "I'm knackered. Give me a minute to catch my breath and we can get rid of the top sheet. I'll have a shower. Care to join me?"

Clay could think of nothing else he'd rather do.

Chapter 6

"We found nothing there that helps tell us what happened to Olivia."
Tate frowned and leaned back in his chair as he observed the crowd
in front of him. He was sitting at his favourite coffee shop in Soho,
enjoying the afternoon sunshine. "Thanks for the loan of the officer."
He and Clay had gone to Olivia's flat earlier this morning before
Clay went to a meeting out of town. It had not been a fruitful visit.

"I know," sighed DS Carol Meadham on the other side of the
line. "My team checked her flat thoroughly too but couldn't find
anything that would show where she'd gone or, in the alternative,
who might have taken her."

"This isn't looking good," Tate said grimly. "She's been missing
for almost a week now and we have no leads, no new ideas." He
picked up his teaspoon and toyed with it. "The posters the guys have
put up have yielded no results and there have been no helpful tips on
the tip line from what you say. It's as if she's disappeared into thin
air." He threw the spoon in the air and caught it deftly. "We haven't
been able to see that friend of Olivia's, Joshua, yet. According to his
employer, he's been unwell, and staying with family, so the owner
said she'd call us back when Joshua is back at work. I'm not sure
how much that'll help, though."

"Hmmm." Carol sounded as frustrated as Tate felt. "My team has
done some door-to-door enquiries in the area she was last seen, as
well as around her flat. No one's seen anything. At least, nothing
they're telling us about. It's looking grim."

"Perhaps you can do one of those re-enactment thingies?" Tate
suggested. "You know, where you retrace her steps, flash her picture
all over the news and see if someone recognises her?"

"I've already sent it to them, plus asked for the local news
channels to broadcast the last CCTV footage we have of her at the
cinema and put out a request for the public to assist with the
enquiries." Carol's voice disappeared as if she was walking around

then returned. "I spoke to DI Grant. He's agreed to speak to a few good mates of his in the newsroom at a couple of the TV channels to get it done ASAP." She sighed heavily. "I can't think of anything else we can do at this stage unless we get any new leads."

Tate nodded. "Sounds like you're doing what you can." He daren't mention that Tomas had created a whole network of people looking out for new information. There were some things the official channels didn't need to know.

"I'll keep you updated," Carol said before she rang off. "If we hear anything, you'll be the first to know."

***

Whatever influence Rick had exercised became evident three days later when several news channels broadcast Olivia's disappearance. As was the nature of the media beast, things were sensationalised to the point they implied some psychotic serial killer had abducted her.

Tate winced when he saw it. Not only was it grossly exaggerated, the press had leapt at the fact she worked in a shop that, according to the media, "was an unusual and eclectic mix of kink and erotica" in an area that offered "anything up to tantalise those looking for something out of the norm." All of which wouldn't endear Aurelio to them. He hated Fetish Alley being in the spotlight, and hated even more his friends and business colleagues being deemed "abnormal."

Tate said as much to Clay when they sat later that evening at home watching the re-run of the day's news. Tate lay down, his head on Clay's lap as he listened to the news programme. Clay's hands threaded through his hair and Tate almost purred.

"Yep, I'm expecting a call from Relio soon," Clay sighed resignedly. "While it's good to have people looking out for Oliva, this might impact negatively on the alley, knowing the bend of small-minded individuals, and he won't like that. It may well mean media and paparazzi lurking around trying to get the inside scoop on all the 'evils that lurk there.'"

Tate agreed. "Double-edged sword," he murmured, closing his eyes and enjoying the warm fingers in his hair. "Public awareness versus the shit storm some people can cause when there's attention on somewhere that doesn't fit into their idea of the perfect world."

An hour later Clay's mobile rang. Tate blinked, the loud ring waking him from a wonderful snooze. He was still prone, his head on Clay's lap, and he sat up woozily, his bones aching and clicking as he did.

Clay grinned at Tate. "Welcome back, sleepyhead. I didn't want to disturb you, lucky for you I didn't need to pee." He answered his phone with a wry smile. "And so it begins. Aurelio? I thought I'd be hearing from you soon." He placed his phone on speaker and laid it down on the table.

Tate muted the TV and sat up to enjoy the upcoming diatribe while wiping the drool from his chin.

That's so not attractive. I bet my hair looks like a scarecrow. He ran a hand over it, trying to shape it into control. Since growing it, it involved so much more maintenance and he'd been tempted to cut it all off again.

"I am not happy with all this media coverage," Aurelio growled. "I understand it had to be done but did these *stronzinos* have to make us look like a bunch of kinky perverts?" He swore loudly. "*Porca miseria.*"

Clay shook his head ruefully. "Relio, it's the media. They'll make sure they overdo it. Don't let them get to you. The important thing is we have eyes out looking for Olivia."

Tomas's voice cut in and Tate assumed he and Aurelio were also on speakerphone. "I have tried to explain this to him," Tomas said aggrievedly. "But he is such a stubborn *zho-pa* and he will not listen to me."

"I listen to you, Tomas," Aurelio hissed. "How can you say such a thing?"

"Huh," Tomas said sulkily. "Maybe in another universe."

Tate chuckled loudly, unable to refrain any longer. "You two lovebirds sound as if things are a little wobbly in paradise. Hashtag relationship problems. Hashtag honeymoon is over."

Clay chuffed in amusement. "Not helping, babe. Relio, things will simmer down soon enough. And think of the publicity being generated for the alley. They say no publicity is bad publicity, right?

"I suppose so," Aurelio muttered grudgingly. "It is annoying that there are people swarming around down here who have no appreciation for my alley and its inhabitants and are only here to see what they can find to make fun of." His voice rose in indignation. "I saw one of Lander's blow-up dolls outside his shop being subjected to certain lewd practices by a group of journalists earlier. These people take nothing seriously."

Tate was trying hard not to laugh too loudly. He'd have paid to see that sight.

"And yet Penny tells me her restaurant is so busy she has a waiting list," Tomas said spiritedly. "So these people are bringing business our way and we have people looking for Livvy. I think that is a winning situation, don't you?"

Clay grimaced. "Really, that awful live food place has a bloody waiting list now?" He shuddered. "Society really has gone screwy."

"Amen," Tate said with fervour. "I couldn't eat anything that talks, wriggles or looks back at me. It's unnatural."

"Well, it's popular," Tomas chimed in. "Don't you watch 'I'm a Celebrity?' The one in the jungle? Those people have to eat the most disgusting things and it's rather funny." He sniggered. "I tried to convince Relio to apply for it, but he's scared and says I must never talk about it again."

"I am not some sideshow carnival to appear on television like a clown," Aurelio said haughtily. "If others wish to make fools of themselves, so be it. This man will not be one of them."

Clay rolled his eyes at Tate. "I'm sure we can live with the disappointment of not seeing you on the telly, Relio." He grinned. "Although seeing you in a loincloth might make quite a conversation starter."

Tate scowled at him. "Really? That's what you get out of this conversation? Aurelio half-naked?"

Clay snorted out a belly laugh. "Babe, you know you're the only one for me."

"I'd like that idea," Tomas murmured. "I've been trying to get Relio to dress up for me, but he refuses. I think the sexy Frank 'n Fruter costume I bought will need to go...mphhh."

It sounded rather as if either a hand or a mouth had silenced Tomas. Tate chuckled and glanced at Clay in amusement.

Clay cocked an eyebrow. "Sounds interesting," he whispered. "Perhaps we should think of doing a little role play?" His fingers reached out and trailed a line of fire up Tate's bare arm. "I rather think I'd enjoy seeing you in a loincloth." His eyes moved suggestively down to Tate's groin which was heating up rapidly as his dick plumped up. Clay traced the outline, and Tate held his breath at the touch.

"You with a sweet bare arse, me with easy access to that lovely cock of yours…" Clay's gaze was intense. "I could so get into that."

Tate swallowed and leaned over to kiss Clay then swore as the phone once again flared into life.

"Gentlemen, I think this conversation is over." Aurelio sounded a little breathless. "I take it you will keep me updated on anything new?"

Clay cleared his throat. "Yes, we'll do that. Enjoy the rest of your day." He ended the call and reached out to pull Tate in for a fierce kiss. Tate was happy to oblige, and his hands slid beneath Clay's polo shirt to find the warm, toned skin.

Tate loved making out on the couch. It took him back to the times when he and Clay had only been friends and done everything together. As Tate explored Clay's mouth, memories of bright, sunshiny afternoons playing video games drifted through his mind. The two of them had known something was happening between them even back when they were teenagers. Clay, however, had been apprehensive about their age gap and unwilling to pursue it further. Instead, he'd signed up for the army and that had been it. They'd stayed in touch, sure, but it hadn't been the familiar, warm relationship they'd enjoyed. Tate imagined it was the same for both of them: awkward, scary, and frustrating.

Then Tate had been shot and Clay arrived back into his life with a vengeance and between them, they'd progressed from old friends to passionate lovers.

The thought Tate now had his man and had no more need to hide how he felt, and had carte blanche to make love to the man in his arms. That comfort Tate now enjoyed was the air that cushioned his life and kept him level.

They stood up urgently, removing all their clothing. Tate knelt on the couch, as Clay worshipped his arse and murmured sweet endearments in his ear. Clay's lean fingers readied Tate for entry, and when that slow slide of Clay's cock made Tate groan and push back, he could have wept for the joy of being so intimate with the man he'd always loved.

The scent of sweat and sex and the way his lover's mouth sought his in desperation played into a medley that was both sensual and sweet. And when the overture sounded and both men roared their satisfaction, Tate once again thanked the stars and the heavens that they'd made it this far together.

***

"Slow down, please Tanvi." Clay stood looking out over the Thames from the tenth floor of the Manchester One building. He'd driven up by car for an appointment because of the inclement weather, currently watching the sheath of rain battering the windows as he tried to calm the agitated woman. "It's bucketing up here, and the line isn't too good. What's this about chocolate?"

"It's about Olivia, someone has sent me a mould..." The line crackled and spit. "There's a letter..." the conversation dropped off and Clay growled in frustration.

"Tanvi, let me call you back from a landline. Give me a minute." Clay disconnected his call and strode around to the phone on the desk. The man sitting behind the desk gestured laconically. He was in his early forties, well built, nattily dressed in a dove grey suit and pink shirt, his shock of grey-white hair slicked back over a high forehead. He rubbed his bearded chin as he observed Clay ruefully.

"Please, use the phone," he drawled as Clay reached into his wallet to take out the business card Tanvi had given him. "I live to serve you."

"Oh can it, Wallace," Clay said good-humouredly as he picked up the phone. "Since when we do we stand on ceremony with one another? I've seen you naked."

And that's another thing I won't share with Tate. Even though it was only in the army barrack showers.

Wallace Merridew had served with Clay back in the day and they'd remained good friends, to the point where Clay was now consulting on an insider trading case Wallace had brought to him.

"And a rare sight that is too, and one you should forever be grateful for," Wallace agreed with a smirk as Clay dialled the number for Chocerotica. Wallace picked up the card and raised an eyebrow. "Do I really want to know?"

Clay ignored him and waited for Tanvi to answer. The phone rang twice then was picked up. "Clay, is that you?" Tanvi's anxious voice echoed down the line.

Clay nodded and tucked the phone against his shoulder as he motioned to Wallace to give him a pen and some paper. "It's me. Now tell me what's going on."

Wallace pushed a pen and a blank page from his notebook in Clay's direction. Clay nodded his thanks.

"This morning I got a letter from whoever has Olivia," Tanvi spluttered.

That comment made Clay's ears prick up. "Is she safe?" were his first words. "What does it say exactly?" He picked up the pen and waited. Wallace tilted his head to one side, gaze watchful.

"That wasn't all he, or she, sent. They also sent a chocolate mould of an ear. Is it hers, do you think? Did they cut it off? Oh my God, what if they did?" The woman's voice spiralled in panic and Clay feared she'd hyperventilate.

"Tanvi, calm down. Let's do this one thing at a time." Clay doubted anyone needed to cut off a person's ear to make a chocolate mould, but that was looking on the bright side. Besides, it could be anyone's chocolate ear. "First read me the letter."

There was the sound of fumbling on the other side then Tanvi's breathless voice reappeared. "It's typed and says, '*I have seen the news and I wish to assure everyone that I would do nothing to hurt Olivia. She is in my possession for safekeeping and will stay that way until I believe it is safe for her to go home. If the authorities will not take care of her, then it is up to me to do so.*" Tanvi stopped, took a breath then read more. "*The chocolate is my offering to prove she is with me. Your forensics can no doubt trace her DNA and prove that this is of Olivia. More will follow as proof she is unharmed until the one troubling her is held accountable for his crimes.*"

Clay looked down his piece of paper and sighed. He'd tried to get the gist of the letter contents down, but it looked like a crazy chicken in flip-flops had walked all over it. "Is that it?"

"Yes, that's all of it. I've saved the envelope and everything for the police, perhaps they can do something with it. Clay, what does this mean? It sounds as if Olivia is okay but what should we do?"

"We pass it onto the cops and let them have a shot at it," Clay said grimly. "We have little choice."

"Okay, I'll call them when we finish here," Tanvi murmured, sounding a little calmer.

Wallace pulled the piece of paper over to him, trying to read it. He shook his head sadly. "Man, you have got no better at that since we were in the military," he mumbled. "You still write like a beetle on crack."

The old idiom had never made sense to Clay, and it still didn't. He laughed briefly then turned the conversation back to Tanvi. "Okay, call DS Meadham, let her know what you've received. Before she takes anything away with her, though, take a few pictures of the envelope, the chocolate mould, and the letter for me. Different angles so Tate and I can work on it too." He hesitated. "I'm thinking whoever has Olivia might be referring to the abusive boyfriend situation. We're going to have to talk to him again. It may be this person holding Olivia has been following him, spying on him even, so perhaps he's noticed something out of the norm."

"You think Olivia is safe, as the person holding her says?" Tanvi's voice cracked.

Clay glanced at Wallace who stared back. "I see no reason to doubt it. It isn't your typical ransom note, so I think for now, yes, she's safe. It could even be someone she knows, man or woman." He frowned. "They sound as if they care about her, which is a good thing."

"That makes me feel a little better." Tanvi sounded relieved. "Fine, I'll go to the police station myself now and drop off this evidence. I'll let you know what they say. Thanks, Clay."

Tanvi rang off and Clay placed the handset back in its cradle. He slumped down into the chair opposite Wallace.

"You able to tell me what that was all about?" Wallace asked as he tapped long fingers on his desk.

Clay shrugged. "A young woman disappeared. We've been searching for her, but the leads have dried up. Today, someone sent a letter saying she's fine, she's only being held for safekeeping. They sent the letter along with a chocolate mould of a woman's ear, ostensibly hers."

His friend's eyes widened. "Hell, that's new. You get the weirdest cases, my friend." He leaned forward in interest. "Any idea what he or she is keeping her safe from? Crazy boyfriend, I gather from your conversation."

"It's possible. We'll look into it again when I get back." Clay rolled his shoulders and winced. "Sorry to detract from what I'm actually here to do. I'll give you a discount."

Wallace guffawed. "That's kind of you, but honestly, don't worry. Young people going missing trumps over a shady character trading shares illegally." He grimaced. "Wait, I retract that word, 'trumps.' Leaves a nasty taste in my mouth. Let's say 'takes precedence' instead."

They got back to business, but all the time Clay's mind was pondering the ramifications of what had happened in Fetish Alley. It sounded as if Olivia was safe for the time being.

He hoped like hell it would stay that way.

Chapter 7

Aurelio took a hit of the joint Tomas passed over to him and inhaled slowly. He passed it back to Tomas, who smiled lazily and raised it to his lips. Aurelio watched in appreciation as Tomas's lips curled around the small cigarette and his cheeks hollowed as he took a pull. It was a look Aurelio loved especially since most times he saw it Tomas was sucking his cock.

"It's good stuff, yes?" Tomas waved the joint around. "After today, I thought we needed a little relaxation." He pushed the bedcovers down to his waist seductively and turned to face Aurelio.

Aurelio grimaced. "Do not remind me. I'm trying to forget everything that happened today. It was, how do you say, a clusterfuck?"

In the previous ten hours, Aurelio had begged the powers that be to smite him down or transport him to another world so he didn't have to deal with people. The only provision he'd given the gods he'd entreated was to ask them to send Tomas along with him for company.

Tomas giggled adorably. "Clusterfuck is putting it mildly." He spluttered with laughter. "I mean, I still can't get over how Cleaver looked when all that shit came shooting out of the drain and covered him." He hooted loudly, his body shaking. "I thought he would cry."

Aurelio sniggered, the soft effect of the weed soaking into his soul and mellowing him. "*Dio mio*, the look on his face when that drain spat back at him, I wish I'd videoed it for YouTube. I think we would have got a million hits."

They were both now laughing uncontrollably, tears streaking their cheeks. "And then when the plumber couldn't stop apologising and was trying not to laugh because Cleaver looked murderous as all hell." Tomas held his sides as his amusement spewed forth much like the contents of the drain the plumber had been trying to unblock. "*O Dieve*, it was too funny."

"Cleaver should have listened when the man told him to step back," Aurelio coughed out in between his laughter. "But you know Cleaver. He has to be, how do you say, the main man."

Tomas passed the joint to Aurelio who took another drag. They grinned at each other and Tomas wriggled closer, his naked body warm and welcoming against Aurelio's. It had been the day from hell but now he had Tomas in his bed, relaxed and, from the way his hard cock pressed against Aurelio's hip, horny as hell.

"Did you sort out the delivery problem?" Tomas murmured as he snuggled closer, his warm fingers under the covers tracing trails down Aurelio's stomach. "I mean, I know people love a bit of fish, but having half a lorry load arrive when you only ordered a few boxes is too much."

Aurelio nodded, his hand gently kneading Tomas's scalp. "Yes, I sent them away, along with the bakery that sent pistachio bread instead of focaccia and the barman who broke a whole tray of gin glasses on his first day in the bar."

Tomas shot up, a frown on his face. "You fired Scotty? That seems harsh, how could you do that to him? He has a family...a little girl and he needs this job."

Aurelio sighed and laid a finger over Tomas's lips. "Hush, *tesoro*. I did no such thing. I asked Siobhan if she needed help in the kitchen because Scotty was a pastry chef at another job, and she agreed to take him on. He's much happier there creating his desserts. Now all I need to do is replace him in the bar."

Tomas sank back down, mollified. "Oh. That's okay then. If you like, I have a friend who might fit in here. She resigned from her old job as a mixologist because the manager kept hitting on her. I'll see if she's interested. "

"Thank you, *cuore mio*." Aurelio smiled at his sexy, naked firebrand. *He is stunning when he gets all het up.*

Tomas fought for the underdogs, people he thought had been wronged and those less fortunate than others. It was one thing he lo...lov—admired—about his lover. Aurelio corrected himself, not wanting to admit to that emotion quite yet. This facet of Tomas was also the one that caused him the most grey hairs. Not that Aurelio would ever tell Tomas that. That was why *Just for Men* was invented. Aurelio was fussy about his fine, head of black hair, and any stray grey strands that found their way into the mix were terminated with extreme prejudice.

The thirteen-year age difference between them rankled Aurelio, especially since he was turning forty next year. Aurelio wasn't sure how he hung onto his young lover but he would make damned sure whatever was between them lasted as long as it could.

"I can hear you thinking, *mylimasis*." Tomas's wicked fingers skated over Aurelio's rapidly inflating cock. "What have I said about bringing your work to bed?"

Aurelio would not reveal what he'd been thinking about. "That when we are in the bedroom, you are in charge. Until you aren't." Aurelio smirked, pulling Tomas closer until he lay on top of him, skin to skin. "Sometimes, seeing you at my mercy, trussed up and naked for me to play with, is what I need. But tonight, I would like it if you took care of me. Made me forget the events of the day and make me come so hard I will need a spaceship to get back down to earth."

Tomas shook his head as he chuckled. "Oh my God, that sounds so cheesy." Despite his comment, his pupils dilated and with the limberness of an alley cat, he climbed aboard the Aurelio Express, straddling his hips. "I think tonight I'll make you scream your release with only my hands," he murmured, as he slicked Aurelio's cock with pre-come and slid his fingers up and down the shaft, like a maestro playing the violin. "A quick fuck is what I need tonight."

Aurelio closed his eyes as Tomas leaned down and his lover's ripe, coffee-scented lips took his in a blistering kiss. A quick fuck was fine by him.

He gasped as Tomas's fingers wrapped around both their cocks and started a rhythm that had him arching his hips up into that firm grasp. Sloppy kisses, moans of pleasure and low sighs accompanied the sound of flesh slicking together. Aurelio's fingers had reached around to Tomas's taut and chiselled backside and he pushed his fingers between Tomas's cheeks, loving the way he squirmed against the onslaught, pushing his arse backwards as if daring Aurelio to enter.

Aurelio couldn't resist a dare, especially when given by a man as sexy as the one who now jerked them both fiercely and swore in his own language—or perhaps it was Russian, Aurelio was never sure—sounding desperate and needy.

"You love it when I stick my fingers in you," Aurelio whispered, as he licked the sweat from Tomas's top lip then bit down gently on the bottom. "You are such a slut for my fingers in your hole. Such a beautiful, needy slut."

The dirty talk was akin to setting a Tomas bomb and watching it going off. As Aurelio pushed two fingers inside the hot, clenching hole of his lover, Tomas shuddered, his body spasming and tightening, like the flesh around Aurelio's fingers. Wetness coated Aurelio's stomach and groin, and he revelled in his own orgasm as Tomas continued to writhe above him.

"God, Relio," Tomas panted, "You are so fucking sexy, I can never get enough of you." Aurelio's fingers withdrew slowly and Tomas collapsed next to him, eyes half-closed, looking shattered.

"I feel the same amount you, *amore mio*," Aurelio murmured. "You are so beautiful when you let go like that and I feel your pleasure right in my soul."

"You are so romantic," Tomas said sleepily, his face wreathed in a goofy smile. "I love that about you."

Aurelio's ears perked at the L-word but he would say nothing right now. Lots of things were said in the aftermath of a man's orgasm.

Tomas's fingers slid across Aurelio's stomach. "Ugh, what a mess. I think a clean-up is necessary before sleep." He turned away and got out of bed. "Don't worry, I'll get something for the mess. You lie there and look gorgeous."

He disappeared into the en suite bathroom and turned on the tap.

Tomas came out with a washcloth, still steaming from the heated water. "Turn back the covers," he instructed. "I'll give you a bed bath." He wiggled his eyebrows salaciously.

Aurelio rolled his eyes but did as he was told. It didn't take long, and they were both clean enough for Tomas to clamber back into bed and attach himself to Aurelio like a limpet. The younger man slept as if he owned the bed, star-fishing across it in the middle of the night.

As they fell into sleep, Aurelio thought it was a small price to pay to have Tomas in his bed, where he belonged.

At least for now.

***

The following morning Aurelio woke to an empty bed and the sound of quiet muttering from the bathroom. He rolled over and squinted at the clock. Eight-thirty in the morning and Tomas was already talking to someone? In the bathroom?

He sighed and heaved himself out of the bed. The bathroom door was ajar, which meant Tomas wasn't doing anything intimate because he had a habit of locking the door when he was. He often went in there to answer his phone, so he didn't disturb Aurelio, who valued his sleep.

Aurelio yawned, knocked once, and pushed the door open. "Tomas, everything okay?"

A naked Tomas looked up at him from where he sat on the side of the jacuzzi bath. He nodded and continued his conversation, louder now, no doubt because Aurelio was evidently awake.

"Tate, I think perhaps we should get together at the club later and go over everything? This new development sounds a little weird."

There was squawking from the other side of the phone and Tomas shook his head impatiently. "I understand. Perhaps after you see him?"

He listened then glanced over at Aurelio. "Fine, I'll text you later. Speak soon." He disconnected the call and stood up. His lithe body called out to Aurelio, and he reached out, hoping to draw Tomas in for a hug and maybe more.

Tomas's eyes glinted. "You'll have to take a rain-check." He grinned cheekily. "We have places to be. There have been developments in Livvy's case." He wandered over to the shower and turned on the water. The rain spray dispersed warm streams and the bathroom mirror began to fog up. "I will shower, without you, and we can get dressed and go down into the club. Tate and Clay will meet us here later this morning after they've interviewed one of Livvy's friends." He stepped into the shower and picked up the gel.

Aurelio sighed. "Fine, *tesoro*." He left Tomas to shower in peace and went to sit on the bed, checking his phone for messages. After they'd both showered and dressed, they left Aurelio's flat to go downstairs.

Cleaver greeted them with a warm smile when they entered the dining room. "Good morning, gentlemen. I have coffee on the table and breakfast will be ready in a while."

Aurelio squeezed Cleaver's massive shoulder as he walked by him. "Thank you, my friend. You are a lifesaver." In more ways than one, he thought. The big man had come into Aurelio's life when he needed it. While the club might employ Cleaver, he was also a good friend. And he'd literally saved Aurelio's life one dark night in Stockholm.

Cleaver grinned widely. "No problem, boss."

Tomas squinted at Cleaver as he perched his backside on one of the dining room chairs. "When are you two going to tell me how you met?" He pouted adorably. "I have asked you both and you are so secretive about it."

Aurelio and Cleaver grinned at each other. "You have an insatiable curiosity about the Cleaver and my antics," Aurelio commented as he sat down next to Tomas. He wasn't a "head of the table" man, plus it took him farther away from his young lover.

"Well, if I don't hear the true story, I can only make it up." Tomas leaned forward and poured him and Aurelio a black coffee. "And my imagination pictures the two of you in the club, doing dirty things to each other. I can't decide who did who though. Aurelio is such a bossy top, and Cleaver, I think you might be a secret lingerie wearer. Lace panties and a camisole." Tomas smirked as Aurelio and Cleaver burst into fits of laughter.

"*Tesoro*, your imagination knows no bounds," Aurelio wiped his eyes as tears streamed from them. "And now I cannot unsee that image you have planted in my brain."

Cleaver shook with amusement. "I don't think they make such things to fit a form like mine." He waved a hand down his large and tall body. "And I'm neither confirming nor denying that assumption, little one. Let that fertile brain of yours work overtime." He sashayed past them, wiggling his ample backside in a show of swish, then waggled his bum in Tomas's face in a parody of a lap dance.

Tomas burst into a fit of giggles and Aurelio's stomach fluttered hearing it. His poor heart was losing itself more and more each day as he grew to love having Tomas in his life. He knew it was probably not forever. Tomas was young and beautiful and there would surely come a time when he'd tire of Aurelio. For now, though, Aurelio basked in the glow Tomas brought to their relationship.

Cleaver disappeared out of the room as Siobhan entered with two plates of Eggs Benedict and placed them on the table. She ruffled Tomas's hair as she walked past and he scowled.

"Do not do that, silly woman. I am not a child."

Siobhan winked at Aurelio, who was trying not to laugh at the injured tone in Tomas's voice. "Oh, get away with you," she sang out in her lilting Irish accent. Aurelio never tired of hearing it. "I have two brothers your age, and they say the same thing to me. It's a sign of affection, *a stór*. Don't go giving me cheek now."

Tomas huffed sulkily, but secretly Aurelio knew he treasured being part of the inner circle here at the club. They all had accepted him into their lives, possibly because they knew Aurelio wished it, so it would be so, but they also liked his lover for who he was.

Breakfast was a quiet affair as Aurelio caught up on world news reading his favourite newspapers and Tomas busied himself reading a book on his Kindle. He was obsessed with horror stories and urban fantasy, gobbling up anything that popped up as recommended on his e-reader. Aurelio hated to think of the amount of money Tomas spent on books.

It was close to mid-day when Clay and Tate finally arrived at the club. Cleaver showed them into the lounge as Aurelio sipped Turkish coffee and Tomas sat at the dining table, muttering to himself as he worked on his laptop. Tomas's eyes brightened as the couple came into the room and he was standing to hug them before they'd even made it halfway in.

"Steady on," Tate grinned when he finally extricated himself from Tomas's octopus hug. "My fiancé's right there. Don't give him the wrong idea."

Clay chuckled as he was subjected to the same treatment. "Don't listen to him. Nowadays I'm lucky to get any attention from another man. They take one look at him," he jerked a thumb in Tate's direction, "and figure out better to play it safe. My man can do fierce scowls like no one else."

Aurelio couldn't resist it. He raised one eyebrow as he shook hands with Tate and gave Clay a brief hug. "Oh? I thought that was his natural expression. I thought perhaps the breeze had changed, and he'd been stuck with that face."

He tried to keep a straight face as Tate gave the scowl he was famous for and showed Aurelio his middle finger. "Fuck you too. And FYI it's the wind that changes a face, not a bloody breeze."

Tomas rolled his eyes and flapped his hand. "You two are like little kittens, snapping at each other. Meow." He folded his long fingers into pretend kitten claws and pawed the air.

Aurelio wasn't sure he wanted to be compared to a kitten, and from the look on his face, Tate wasn't a fan either. Luckily Clay stepped in, ever the pacifier.

"I'm sure we came here to give you an update, not have a pissing contest. Can we get back to that?"

He snorted and sat down in an easy chair, crossing his long legs casually. Aurelio might have been with Tomas now, but he still remembered the days when those strong legs of Clay's had been wrapped elsewhere. He mentally shook himself. *Not acceptable. That part of my life is over and I have my fierce little cockerel now.* The man who brought the heat to his groin, a strange swell of affection to his chest and drove him crazy as no one had ever done before. Even Clay.

Clay raised one eyebrow at him. "Relio? You gonna stand there all day?"

Aurelio came to his senses, realising he was the only one still standing. He cleared his throat and sat down on the couch, next to Tomas. "My apologies. Please, tell us what happened. I assume Olivia is still missing?"

Clay nodded, face grim. "Yes. But someone has contacted the police and Tanvi, and it seems she's safe." He gave a succinct update of latest events, the details of which Aurelio reeling in disbelief.

"It sounds like something out of a detective novel," he murmured. "Chocolate moulds?"

"Well, yeah, you know," Tate remarked sarcastically, as he waggled a finger between him and Clay, "because, detectives, you know?"

Aurelio stared at him frostily. "Investigators, actually. At least that's what Clay always takes great pains to explain to me. He doesn't seem to like the word detective being used."

"Yeah, because he always thinks of tweed caps and long coats when he hears that word," Tate chortled. "Investigators is more 'corporate.'" He made air quotes with his fingers then groaned 'Ouch, that hurt" as Clay tweaked the skin under Tate's arm.

"Can we please get back to the update instead of having this highly educational conversation?" Clay demanded with a fierce stare around the room. "I have a meeting later this afternoon and I'd like to be on time for it."

Aurelio inclined his head regally. "As you wish. First, tell me, how does a person go about making moulds of people's body parts, anyway?"

Clay grinned. "I thought you'd never ask." He hitched his backside onto the arm of the chair Tate sat in. "We had a rather interesting YouTube education with Tanvi into how this is all done. There are a couple of ways you can do it. There's this stuff called…" he stopped and glanced at Tate, "What was it called again?"

"Body Double silicone rubber, or something like that," Tate supplied helpfully.

"Right. It's quite a lengthy process to do these moulds, and you have to put cream on the person being moulded so the silicone stuff sticks to it and it protects the person's skin plus allows the rubber to peel off easily. Then you make up the rubber gunk, smear it all over the face, or whatever and let it dry."

Aurelio frowned. "Sounds like a long, drawn-out process."

Clay nodded. "It is. That's not the end. You have these wet bandages you apply to this face that dries like paper maché. That can take fifteen to twenty minutes. You then remove the shell and peel off the rubber mask."

Tate chipped in. "You stick the mask into the support shell, which is the paper maché thingy, and then voila! You have a mould you can pour melted chocolate into and make a face."

"That sounds like a lot of trouble for a kidnapper to do to get a point across," Tomas said, who had been sitting listening in fascination. Aurelio agreed.

"We thought so too. But Tanvi said there was another way, but it was way expensive." Clay replied. "There's something new out there apparently, Tanvi explained it like one of those puzzle things which is made of nails and when you put your hand in or whatever, it forms the shape of that thing?"

"You mean 3-D pin art?" Aurelio said drily. "Yes, I know of this thing."

"Glad you knew what the fuck he was talking about," Tate muttered. "I had to Google it."

Clay chuckled. "Well, it's the same premise. You have this thin block of silicone rubber, heat it in the microwave to make it pliable and then place it over the thing you want a mould of. It does the job all in one, no mess no fuss."

"We thought if this person cares for Olivia as he or she says he does, they probably wouldn't want to put her through all the fuss of doing it the long way, plus the fact, why the hell would she sit still while someone messes with her, so perhaps they might have bought some of these moulds." Tate stood up and stretched. "It's a long shot, but Rick and his team are looking into it. It's expensive stuff, sold only at select shops, so it narrows it down a bit."

Relio rubbed his chin thoughtfully. "It is something to consider." A sliver of hope sliced through him. At this stage, they'd need to take any bit of hope they could in finding the missing Fetish Alley worker.

Aurelio couldn't resist what came next. "Perhaps we could commandeer some of this special moulding and make a mask of your face, Tate," he said wickedly. "I'm sure we could use them for Halloween masks next year."

"Ha bloody ha," Tate sniped back. "You think you're so clever."

Aurelio sniggered as Clay burst into laughter. Tomas, who'd been immersed in his laptop, snickered quietly. "You guys make me wish I wasn't leaving for home soon. I like listening to you all bicker." He looked at Tate. "That is the right word, yes? Bicker?"

As Tate nodded his head, Aurelio felt as if he'd been poleaxed. "Wait a minute," he said. "You're leaving to go to Lithuania?" It was news to him.

Tomas had the grace to look guilty, but his chin rose defiantly. "My flight leaves at ten o'clock tonight. I have some personal business to attend to."

"And I'm only learning this now?" Aurelio's chest hurt and he clenched his fists. "When were you going to tell me?"

Tomas's eyes drifted to Tate's. "I've been meaning to say something, but then Olivia disappeared and," he shrugged, "I forgot. I'm sorry." He turned his head back down to his laptop screen. A shock of dark brown hair fell, obscuring his face.

"I see." Aurelio wanted to take this further, but Tate and Clay were looking uncomfortable and he would rather discuss his private issues with Tomas when they were alone. But he couldn't resist a parting comment. "Well, thank you for letting me know. Although I hate to think what would have happened had you not mentioned it now. Would you have disappeared?"

Tomas's bright blue eyes rose to meet his. "I would have told you, not slipped away like a thief in the night, Relio."

Aurelio clenched his jaw, frustration swelling in his chest. "You've done it before. I suppose I shouldn't be surprised." Two months ago, Tomas had disappeared for almost five days. He'd been seconded to some corporate task squad to help them with some security issues. While there, he'd been unable to communicate, and forgotten to tell Aurelio before being bundled up in a helicopter and flown off to God knows where. It had all been highly secretive. Aurelio had been frantic with worry.

Tomas's face darkened. "Why did I know you would bring that up?" He swore to himself in what Aurelio imagined was Lithuanian or perhaps Russian. Tomas's other go-to language when he was angry. "I explained myself then. Do you have to keep holding that over my head like some cardinal sin?" He jumped up and closed his laptop, placing it on the side table. He glared at Aurelio who glared back.

Clay coughed softly and stood up. "Well, we've done what we came for, so I think we'll be off now. Given what was said in the letter about keeping Olivia safe. Tate and I think it might be the boyfriend the kidnapper is trying to save her from. It's all we've got to go on right now. We're heading down to speak to him again, see if he has anything new to share." He cleared his throat. "We've asked Tanvi if Olivia appeared to have anyone protective of her or was stalking her because that's what it sounds like, but she couldn't come up with any one specific. It's a mystery."

Tate nodded. "Given the fact this person who has Olivia is concerned about the boyfriend abuse, Rick and his team have also widened their net to include abused men and women Olivia may have met who could have empathy with what she was going through. Perhaps Olivia contacted the Samaritans or a woman's help organisation at some stage." He shrugged. "They found no evidence of such in her flat but it's worth a look into." He stood up and collected his jacket from the seat beside him where it lay, casting an amused glance at Tomas. "Looks like you two have something to resolve without us here."

"If anything else happens, I'll call you," Clay promised as he made his way toward the door. "Don't worry about seeing us out, I'm sure we can find our own way."

Aurelio had never seen two men beat such a hasty retreat. He waited until they'd closed the door behind them, then sank down into his chair. "Is everything okay back home, Tomas?"

Tomas pressed his lips together and didn't answer. He tucked his laptop under his arm and took a few steps toward the side door.

Aurelio sighed. "*Tesoro*, I wish to understand what is happening in your life. I do not wish to be possessive but I am wounded you felt it necessary to share your departure with me only now."

Tomas turned back and clicked his tongue in irritation. "I told you, I forgot. Now you know, I don't see what the problem is." He huffed. "I need to go pack."

"How long will you be away?"

Tomas shrugged. "I'm not sure. My friend is very ill. Our foster family wishes for me to be there for him."

Aurelio's eyes widened. "Your foster family? I did not know you had one." Another secret Tomas had kept. His secrecy vault must surely be overflowing by now. *Madre de Dio*, Aurelio thought. Will he ever trust me completely to let me in on his past?

"I was a visitor there for many years before I moved on. My friend's name is Valentin." Tomas whispered. "He's a year younger than me and needs me there. His foster family is good to him, but they cannot support him like I can in this." His eyes darkened and Aurelio's throat choked up.

How ill was Valentin to produce that look of sadness in Tomas's eyes?

"I could help," Aurelio murmured. "That's what partners are for. To support each other, help one another get through tough times."

Tomas shook his head. "I need to do this on my own. With Valentin. He has…issues. Ones that make him distrust strangers."

He turned to leave and Aurelio watched helpless as Tomas left.

When he got to the door, he turned but didn't look at Aurelio. "I am sorry I didn't tell you earlier. Please, could you keep in touch with me about any progress on Olivia's case while I am gone? I would appreciate it."

Then he was out the door which snicked closed behind him. Aurelio took a deep breath, lay back and shut his eyes. From the tone of that last request, it sounded as if Tomas would pack and then make his way to the airport. Alone, independent, and apart.

Cristo, but the man drove Aurelio to drink with Tomas's unrelenting need for keeping his private life so close to his chest. Aurelio knew what he'd been getting into with the mysterious, yet sexy and passionate hacker. Being ignored and relegated to things on a "need to know" basis seared his possessive Italian soul.

"Well, if you think you are leaving here without a proper goodbye, you are mistaken, *tesoro*," Aurelio said grimly to himself. He stood up and paced toward the door. "There is no way you are leaving here without one."

When Aurelio reached their shared bedroom fifteen minutes later, frustrated from being stopped with menial requests and discussions of menus and visitor lists as he made his way through the club, Tomas was gone. His backpack, toiletries, favourite sweatshirt, and the dog- eared book he'd been reading, which normally resided on his bedside table, were nowhere to be seen.

Chapter 8

Clay had always loved the snow. He loved the way it fell from the skies, soft and powdery, landing on the earth to cover it with white crystal perfection. It brought back memories of his childhood, when he and Tate had built snowmen, using remnants of old clothing found in the recycling bags to dress them. A scarf here, an old tweed cap there and their masterpiece had been completed.

Clay's favourite memory of them together in the snow had been when he'd been around seventeen, not long before he'd signed up for the army. Tate had been fourteen then, all gangly limbs and deep hazel eyes and Clay remembered wanting to kiss him so badly, it had become a craving he'd had to physically suppress. His growing sexual attraction to Tate, all five foot eight of him, his sharp tongue, his quick wit, and his wide smile was Clay's Kryptonite.

They'd been laughing and snowballing each other, both soaked with snow crystals and Tate had run after Clay, pushing him down into the snow and straddling him, while trying to stuff a snowball into his jeans. The feel of Tate's hands on him, the closeness of his body, the way Tate's hands had found Clay's skin, his fingers frozen but warming Clay as if a furnace had been lit inside him.

Clay had wrested control from Tate, rolling them both over again and clambering off Tate so quickly Clay thought he'd pulled a muscle. That would have been preferable to Tate feeling what lay beneath Clay's jeans: a boner so hard and needy that had Tate felt or seen it, Clay would have been mortified.

They'd stopped the snowball fight then, Clay choosing instead to challenge Tate to make a snow angel and see who could make the best one.

Now, he smiled as he looked outside the window at the garden, seeing the soft flakes settle, obliterating the green grass and nodding pansies under a thin blanket of white.

"Here you go. One hot chocolate with marshmallows." Tate handed Clay a steaming mug. The scent of warm gooey goodness coupled with the fragrant cocoa tantalised Clay's nostrils. He inhaled, and heaved a satisfied sigh, "Ahh, thanks, babe. Did you bring the shortbread biccies too?"

Tate snorted and tossed a half-eaten packet of biscuits onto the lounge table. He quirked an eyebrow at Clay. "More than my life's worth to forget your shortbread. Knock yourself out." He chuckled as Archie got out of his basket by the fireplace and trotted over. The pup loved sweet stuff and biscuits were one of his favourites. Keeping his eyes on the biscuits, then offering a soulful gaze at Tate, Archie snuggled in under Clay's feet, his little tongue hanging out in a doggy smile.

Clay reached down and scratched Archie between his ears, as the pup rolled over, offering his belly. "You are such a tart," Clay murmured as he rubbed fingers along the furry little belly. "Look at you as if butter wouldn't melt in your mouth."

On the couch, Tate cradled his drink, long legs stretched out in front of him. He too had easy access to Archie's tummy, and the pup closed his eyes in ecstasy as his two owners spoilt him. "I swear, this is the most snow we've had in ages," Tate said. "The bookies are forecasting a white Christmas."

Clay narrowed his eyes and stared out as he sipped his chocolate. "They say that every year, though." He sighed. "Snow isn't like it used to be when you and I were younger. Then we had snow days and two feet of the stuff. Now with global warming and all that crap, we have less of it, only enough to cock things up with the trains and motorways." He trailed off as a robin came and perched on the denuded Japanese maple tree a few feet away. "Hey, there little fellow. There's no food on that branch, go over to the feeder station, lots to choose from there." The robin cocked his head to the side, then, as if it'd heard Clay, darted over to the feeder and began pecking daintily at the seed. Clay smiled in triumph.

"He talks to birds and they listen," Tate murmured as he dunked a biscuit into his chocolate. "Perhaps we should call you Doctor Dolittle." He stared over at Archie, curled in his basket, fast asleep. "What do you think, Arch? Can you understand what he says?"

At the sound of his name, Archie opened one eye, cast a bleary glance at them, and went back to enjoy his belly rubs, not before he cast another longing glance at the biscuit packet.

Clay grinned and plonked down into the chair, reaching over for the biscuits. "I'm full of talents, me. Including magic. I can make things disappear." He shovelled half of the biscuit into his mouth and offered the other half to Archie, who took it gently and nibbled on it.

"I hope it lets up for this afternoon." Tate scrunched up his nose. "We've got to go visit Joshua Bradford later today. I don't fancy riding on the bike in this weather if we can help it. The train might be a better bet if they're still running."

Clay nodded. "Agreed. We should be okay. I checked. The line's been running fine today, and where Joshua works isn't too far from the tube station." He frowned. "I'd been hoping to get more information out of the douchebag we saw the other day, her boyfriend, but he appears truly clueless."

Clay still had a gut feeling the whole kidnapping thing had something to do with Allan Smith and him abusing Olivia, but the young man had refused to admit he'd ever done anything wrong.

Tate nodded. "He's definitely a bully, and a little shit, and Olivia is no doubt better off without him, but that doesn't leave us with anything tangible as to who might have Olivia. Rick was arranging a more in-depth interview of the guy down at the police station. I think Carol was doing the grilling."

Both men sniggered at that. DC Carol Meadham was a master at interrogation and if anyone could get anything concrete out of Allan Smith, it was her. Stupid sod was in for a rough ride.

They sat in comfortable silence and contemplated the weather. Inside was toasty warm, the central heating adding an air of satisfying comfort in opposition to the chill outside.

"Remember the old days?" Tate remarked softly. "We used to have snowball fights and build snowmen. We haven't done that in ages." His gaze outside grew contemplative. "Those were good times."

"We were teenagers." Clay took another biscuit from the packet and bit down on it. Archie sat up hopefully, but Clay shook his head. "No more for you, little one. Too much isn't good for you." Archie whined and lay back down as Clay chewed his biscuit. "Back then, all we thought about was sex, beer, and pizza. In that order."

Tate snorted. "Yeah. I know I was horny most of the time, especially around you." He glanced at Clay, a look of rueful admission on his face. "As I said before, back then I wasn't sure how you felt about me, so I kinda suppressed it and did nothing about it." He flashed a cheeky grin at Clay. "Now look at us. Five years together as a couple and still going strong."

The nostalgia in his lover's tone gave Clay an idea. He stood up and reached across for Tate's hand. "Come on."

Tate grasped Clay's hand, his face curious. "Where are we going?"

Clay pulled him to his feet and pulled him toward the back door in the kitchen. "You'll see." Archie watched them curiously but made no move to follow. He wasn't a fan of snow and had objected vocally when Tate had taken him out to play. The pup had taken one step outside, howled pitifully and then dashed back into the house.

As they passed the coat rack on the wall outside the kitchen, Clay plucked Tate's jacket off the hook. "Gloves might come in handy too. You still got them in your jacket pocket?"

Tate nodded in bemusement. "I always keep my gloves in there. What the fuck is going on?"

Clay shrugged into his own jacket and slid his hands into his gloves. "Time to make some new snow memories." And this time neither of us needs to hold anything back.

He tugged a confused Tate out into the darkened back garden, propelling him toward the middle, where the snow lay thickest and pristine. With one quick, fluid movement, Clay had Tate on his back on the ground, as Tate gave a startled squawk.

"What the fuck?" Tate lay staring up at Clay, who straddled him and grinned down at the man who held his heart.

"Like I said, time to make some new memories. We've never made out in the snow before and you confessed you had a fantasy about it.so…"

Tate's eyes darkened, and Clay leaned down and pressed his lips to his lover's. The chemistry between them had always been strong, but tasting the coffee and cherry cold drops Tate loved to suck on lips that opened willingly beneath Clay's and with much hunger, he was transported back to those days when they'd been younger and foolish, not giving in to whatever was between them.

Clay's mouth fought with Tate's for dominance and he held Tate's hands above him in the snow. Under him, Tate's body pressed urgently up into Clay's and as the kiss ended and they lay spent in the cold. Tate smiled up at him.

"Wow," he murmured, eyes shining. Clay could look into those toffee flecked eyes all day and never get tired. Tate's eyes were among the most expressive Clay had ever seen. Tate's soul shined through. "Look at you being Mr Romantic. I like it."

Clay was so caught up in that moment, he seemed surprised when Tate wrenched his hands-free and turned the tables, Clay was on his back, Tate perched on top of him.

Tate grinned in victory and brushed the scruff of his chin across Clay's throat as he trailed a warm lick down Clay's throat. "Gotcha," he declared as his tongue laid trails of fire on Clay's skin. "I would normally continue down and take your cock in my mouth but I'm afraid out here in the cold I might not find it…." He laughed loudly at his own joke, a sound soon stopped as Clay grabbed a handful of snow in his fist and pushed the icy ball into Tate's face. Tate gave a surprised shout, then leapt to his feet as agile as a cat. "So that's where we're going with this?" he taunted as he scooped snow into a gloved hand and cast it Clay's way. "Snowball fight? You'll lose."

Clay huffed as he built a mega snowball. "Says you. I'll teach you to make fun of my bits."

Ten minutes later, exhausted, soaking wet, and deliriously happy, Clay laid down to make a snow angel. Tate was next to him, arms stretched wide, as their legs pistoned in tandem. They were both panting, breaths of white air puffed above them into the flakes of snow falling from the tree that scattered lazily down to rest on their bodies.

"I think it's time for another mug of hot chocolate," Clay puffed as he stopped his cardiovascular exercise and looked up at the grey sky. "At this rate, we'll both get pneumonia."

"Don't be such a fucking softy," Tate scoffed as he too stilled. "But hot choc sounds like a good bet to me." He got to his feet, extending a hand to Clay. He took it and Tate pulled him up then pulled him close for a hug. "Thanks for this," Tate said gruffly, as his scruff brushed against Clay's cheek. "I like these new memories." His cold lips touched Clay's briefly, and he turned to go back inside. As soon as he walked toward the house, Clay sniggered and bent down to make another mega snowball. As silently as he could, he approached Tate, knowing he'd have to run fucking fast once his job was done.

Clay yanked back the hood of Tate's jacket and thrust the snow down Tate's back. Tate shouted, "You fucker, wait 'til I get you," as Clay sprinted for the door and disappeared inside. He nearly tripped over Archie waiting patiently by the door for the men to come in from the horrible white stuff. Archie barked shrilly and bounded around joyfully.

"Come on, little guy, let's go get warm before he comes in and tries to maim me." Clay hung his soaking wet jacket and gloves on the rack. "And perhaps you can have another bit of biscuit seeing as how you didn't join in the fun outside."

Tate stormed in, shaking his hair and doing a jerky dance as he tried to dislodge the freezing snow against his skin. "You bastard," he hissed, as he pulled off the wet clothing. "I owe you one for that and make no mistake, I'll make you bloody pay."

"Ooh," Clay said as he started to prepare the new drinks. "I'm shaking in my boots, babe."

"You should be," Tate muttered grimly, but Clay saw the amusement on his face. "Arch, your dad has been a bad boy. Should we send him to the naughty corner?"

"I can think of other ways to punish me," Clay murmured as he stirred the milk on the stove. "Use your imagination. I'm sure something will come up."

Tate snorted but his gaze heated. "I think the stuff coming up that you have in mind is more of a reward than a punishment. For both of us." He reached down and picked up the pup who squirmed in his arms, trying to lick the skin from Tate's face.

Clay finished making the hot chocolate in a haze of content. It might have been cold outside, but inside, their home was warmer than anywhere he'd ever been.

***

Clay sat back in his chair in the small waiting room at the shop called Chocolate Heaven as he and Tate listened to its proprietor, Hazel, give him some advice on how best to communicate with Joshua Bradshaw.

"He's an introvert," she explained. "Socially awkward, extremely private and he doesn't do small talk. He has a tough time connecting with strangers. It took me a while, but he's come around. He's a good employee, he works in the factory at the back, packing and making sure things run smoothly. He has incredible attention to detail, and he's not a fan of people, so being hidden away is where he prefers to be." She wrinkled her nose. "He's not a fan of handshaking, so don't offer."

Clay nodded. "Good to know. I assure you we'll be respectful of those things and try not to upset him. All we want to ask is whether he's seen Olivia lately or if he knows where she is. You understand, we have to follow up every lead we have."

"It's a dreadful state of affairs," Hazel said sadly. "He doesn't really talk about Olivia much, although I know he enjoys going to the other shop to see her." She smiled at them. "He's waiting in my office for you." She waved at a small room behind the storefront. "I'll be back in a while. Customers to see out there."

Hazel disappeared and Tate and Clay walked into the office to see a young man sitting in the visitor's chair. Joshua Bradford was a slightly built man with sleek blond hair and a long, pale face speckled with freckles and acne scars.

Clay drew up a chair, keeping a respectful distance, and sat down, smiling over at Joshua. Tate perched his backside on the desk and waited. Clay noticed with amusement Tate kept his arms uncrossed, letting them linger at his sides. He looked a little uncomfortable but no doubt he didn't want Joshua feeling intimidated. Body language was an important consideration when dealing with skittish people.

"Good afternoon, Joshua, thanks for seeing us," Clay said, leaning back in his chair comfortably. "We'll try not to keep you too long, I promise. We want to ask some questions about Olivia."

Joshua looked up, his green eyes wary. "What sort of questions?"

"Routine ones to see if you might have noticed anything different about her the last time you saw her. Is that all right?"

Joshua hesitated then nodded.

"Do you remember when you last saw Olivia?" Clay asked.

Joshua nibbled at a fingernail. "I went to her shop to buy some chocolate. It was last week sometime."

"Can you remember the day?" Tate asked gently. "That would help us a lot. Please take your time."

Joshua frowned. "I bought Turkish Delight so it must have been Wednesday. I always buy that on Wednesdays. She packed it for me in a blue bag. Olivia knows I like blue." Joshua lifted his hand, splayed his fingers and stared at them intently, turning his hand from side to side.

"That helps. Did you ever see Olivia with anyone who might have upset her, been a little too protective?"

Joshua's gaze shot up to Clay's. "No," he said shortly. He nibbled on his fingernail again.

"Do you have any thoughts about her whereabouts, somewhere she may have gone to get away?" Tate cleared his throat.

Joshua stared down at the floor. "No," he mumbled. "I don't think so." He frowned at the tableau outside the shop window and seemed not to like what he saw.

Clay glanced outside to see two children playing on the pavement in the snow. The shop was in a quiet cul-de-sac off the high street, and the kids appeared to be having a good time, albeit getting wet as they threw snowballs at each other.

"They shouldn't be out there in the snow. It's too cold for them," Joshua mumbled.

Tate chuckled. "They're kids having fun, and it's not as if we get this much snow each year. Didn't you ever play out in the snow as a child like that?"

Joshua didn't answer, but cast a scornful glance at Tate from under sandy eyelashes.

There was a knock on the door and Hazel appeared. "You gentlemen okay here?"

Joshua nodded and went back to staring outside, rubbing his fingers against each other.

"We're good, thanks. I don't think we have anything else to ask Joshua." Clay glanced at Tate, who shrugged. It looked like they'd learnt all they could for now.

"It's scary that someone can go missing like Olivia has," Hazel continued. "I mean, who knows what sort of monster has her in his clutches, or whether she's still alive? We all read the newspapers and whoever has her, I hope we find them soon." She waved a hand angrily. "They ought to burn in hell for what they've done if you ask me."

Clay noticed Joshua's shoulders stiffen and his hands clench in his lap. His agitation was palpable, and Hazel's words didn't seem to have helped.

"We don't know for sure anyone's taken her," Tate remarked softly. He gave Hazel an apologetic grin. "Probably better to stay positive and not think the worst yet." He inclined his head toward Joshua and Hazel's eyes widened in concern.

"Oh, I'm sorry. I'm concerned about her, that's all. I didn't think about…" She looked at Joshua, her face flushing.

Clay tried to reassure her. "I know you're worried. That's why we'll keep asking questions until something comes to light and in the meantime, we'll hope for the best." He turned back to the young man now sitting staring into space, his gaze unfocused. "Joshua, if she contacts you, could you let us know?"

Joshua ignored them at first, then after a minute, he nodded. "Fine, I'll do that," he replied, sounding bored. "Can I go back to work now? I have a ton of things to do."

Clay nodded. "Thank you for talking to us."

Joshua stood up in one quick movement and disappeared into the back of the shop, firmly closing the heavy door behind him.

"I'm sure if he hears anything from Olivia, he'll let me know," Hazel continued. "We've built up a good relationship and he doesn't have a lot of family support, so I try to help him." She scowled. "His mother is too flighty and can't bother with him, and his dad is always off somewhere in the world for his business."

"Does he live at home with them?" Tate asked curiously.

Hazel shook her head. "No. He has his own home close to here. His parents bought him this rather large basement flat in Shepherds Green, probably to get rid of their guilt that they hadn't been more supportive." She snorted. "He manages well but I think it's a lonely life. He lives for his work here. It's why he and Olivia seemed to hit it off. She's kind, sweet and never seemed to look down on him like others do because he's a bit of an introvert, like her. When she came into the shop that first day they met, she made him laugh. That's a tough thing to do, trust me."

Clay and Tate stood up and Clay smiled at her. "If we hear anything about the case, I promise we'll be in touch."

They left the shop no wiser about anything than when they'd entered. As they walked back toward the station down the busy high street, Tate stopped and gestured to a nearby streetlamp.

"The lads have been busy," he remarked as they walked over to see the "Have You Seen This Woman?" posted tacked to the post. Olivia's face stared out at them, wet from the snow and looking rather bedraggled. "They printed off hundreds of these and put them all over the city. Let's walk back through the alley to the tube, perhaps we'll run into one of them and we can say thanks for the help." He sounded proud of his graffiti buddies, Josiah and friends, and Clay held back a grin. His man was like a doting father.

"I'm not getting a good vibe from this at all," Clay confessed. "We have virtually nothing to go on, none of the activity Rick and his team have brought any new leads, despite all the CCTV footage and the house to house enquiries. It's as if we're pissing in the bloody dark," he muttered in irritation. "The silicone mould leads didn't turn up anything we could use. I'm thinking on this one we're losing our touch." He snorted. "The only good thing to happen so far isn't related to this case. Did I tell you the Midlands team found the leak of the person who revealed Smokey D's whereabouts?"

Tate turned to stare at him. "No, you didn't. Who was it?"

"It was one of the junior police constables out the Bristol office who inadvertently let the location slip to a news journalist covering the court story. That little snippet found its way into the news with no one being aware. I've already hauled them over the coals about it. They should have been monitoring the newspapers and channels. A man died because of their carelessness."

Tate rolled his shoulders, a familiar way he had of easing the tension in his body. "That fucking sucks, although I'm glad they plugged the leak." He cleared his throat. "Coming back to our case. Rick's got the forensics team on the chocolate, and the note and last time I spoke to him, they had nothing to go on. We can only hope something comes up and keep searching. Something has to give."

He didn't sound so sure. Clay had done his research on missing people many a time and he knew the statistics weren't good. "There's this charity called Missing People, and I read a report recently that one hundred and eighty thousand people are reported missing every year in the UK. That's one every ninety seconds. One in two hundred children will go missing, with that number standing at one in five hundred for adults. In London alone, missing person cases have increased seventy-seven per cent since 2010. So no, the prognosis isn't all that good."

"It's fucking depressing if you ask me," Tate growled as they walked into Fetish Alley. "Why d'you have to tell me that shit?" He kicked moodily at a beer can lying on the cobbled street. Then, with a huff, he walked over, picked it up and dropped it into a rubbish bin. "People leaving their fucking litter all over the place. I'd like to stuff it down their gullet. I mean, is it too damned difficult to toss it in there?" He motioned to the bin. "Jesus, some people."

"Babe, calm down," Clay said with a chuckle. "You're scaring the public with that scowl on your face."

Tate forged on ahead, ignoring Clay, who sighed and followed him. They were passing the shop E-Lixer when someone hailed them.

"Hello there, Mr Mortimer, could I talk to you please?"

Clay turned to see Eleanor Lixer hurrying over to them, her usual blue Fedora perched on top of her red curls. He smiled at her as she reached them. "Ms Lixer. Lovely to see you again." He noticed that Tate held back, nodding cursorily at Eleanor but not getting too close. Tate was a little in awe of the woman, given her uncanny way of saying things that seemed to resonate with him.

"I'm well, thank you. I had to chat with you about Olivia." Her voice was a little breathless and Clay knew she'd seen them pass by and hurried out to find them.

"Olivia? You have some news about her whereabouts?"

Eleanor looked at him with wide green eyes. "No, but I had a vision. I woke up last night, from a strange dream and I had to share it with you. I had a feeling I'd be seeing you today."

Tate shuffled forward. "Was this meeting in your dream, then?" His gaze met Clay's stare and Tate mouthed "What?" as if asking made him as strange as Eleanor.

Eleanor laughed, a tinkling sound that made Clay think of Christmas troika bells. "Heavens, no. I'm not that psychic. Hazel told me you were coming to see Joshua, and I thought you might come down the alley. You usually do when you visit someone around here."

Tate looked a little crestfallen. No doubt the fact he and Clay were predictable wasn't as exciting as a psychic seeing the future.

"Anyway," Eleanor continued, "I keep seeing an ear. A woman's ear. Oh, and a hand. I don't know what significance they have, but I think they belong to Olivia."

Clay's spine tingled. The chocolate ear and the mould with the note hadn't been released to the public. It was being kept quiet so they could identify the real killer later, and so Rick's team wouldn't have to fend off the crank callers on the tip line. There was no way Eleanor could have known about it. From the expression on Tate's face, he'd come to the same conclusion.

"An ear?" Clay repeated carefully. "That's hmm, interesting. Do you know its significance?"

Eleanor shook her head, her dangling earrings flying about like miniature hoops on a wire. "I have no clue. I feel that Olivia is safe, though, there's this warmth about wherever she is that tells me she's being looked after." Her face fell. "I understand that isn't particularly useful, but surely it means something. Whoever has her, if that's what happened, is taking good care of her?"

Tate cleared his throat. "That's a good feeling to have. Did your, err, dream give you any indications about who may have her, or where she might be? Were there any sounds in your dream that may prove useful?"

Eleanor's brow furrowed as she thought. "I only saw flashes of the ear and hand, which I knew was hers, because it had a ring on it, a thin gold band on the middle finger, with a tiny stone in it. It was an amethyst ring her parents gave her years ago." She smiled happily. "The amethyst is a stone that helps mental healing and creates spiritual light around the body. It protects the wearer." She looked at them both hopefully. "I hope this helps. I feel so useless not being able to see more, but unfortunately, that's how my gift works. It only shows me random things." She fiddled with the beads around her neck. "Has your other psychic friend been able to help in any way?"

Clay assumed she was referencing Taylor. Word had got around in the alley of his help on the last case and he'd become something of a talking point.

"Yeah, Tay went to her flat and did his spooky mind meld thing," Tate said. "But as we've no crime scene and nothing to give him to go on, he didn't pick much up. He tried touching a scarf of hers which gave him a sense of who she was, and like you, he thought she was safe. That was about it." He shrugged. "You've given us more than he could. I guess it's your personal connection."

Clay nodded at that and reached out a hand to clasp Eleanor's. He felt a slight tingle, but attributed it to static. "Thank you for telling us. At this stage, we'll take anything we can get, no matter how random it is."

Eleanor beamed. "I'm glad I could do something. Have you seen all the wonderful posters Josiah and his crew have been putting up? They worked at it all night again last night printing more out and tacking them up everywhere."

Tate grinned. "Yes, in fact, we were on our way to see them and say thanks. They've done a great job." He glanced at Clay. "We'd better get on. We appreciate the info, Eleanor."

Ten minutes into their journey meandering through the alley— Tate had stopped to buy them food and something to quench their thirst—they found Josiah and Freddy sitting sprawled against a wall, debating something heatedly. It sounded like an argument about who produced the best burgers.

Josiah sprang to his feet when he saw them, a huge grin on his face. "What's up, dudes?" Tate and he did this silly handshake thing that for the life of him Clay couldn't master and didn't want to. Josiah brushed wispy brown hair away from his face and gestured to Freddy. "Stand up and say hi, man. Aincha you got no manners?"

Freddy threw him a finger but rolled his lanky body up and did the same handshake thing with Tate. "Haven't seen you guys in a while," he observed. "You down here checking on Olivia's case?"

Tate nodded. "Thought we'd come by and say thanks to you and your crew for putting up the posters. You guys rock."

Josiah flushed, his pale, acne-scarred face turning pink. "Isn't anything someone else wouldn't have done. Olivia's one of our own. We need to find her."

Freddy nodded, his dreadlocks bouncing around his face. "Yeah, man. It's not cool she's still missing. She's a nice lady." Clay was glad Freddy hadn't said, "was." It seemed there was still hope among people in the alley for her reappearance.

"Everyone is doing their best," Clay assured the pair. "It sucks that it's taking so long. The police are following up on some new leads so things are happening."

Josiah mock punched Tate in the arm. "I know you guys will do everything you can. Tate here is my man." He gestured at a wall behind him. "Hey, haven't seen you down here creating any art lately. You too good for us now?"

Tate laughed. "Hell, no. It's been fucking busy and time's got away with me. I promise I'll come down as soon as I get a spare moment."

"You make sure you do." Freddy snorted. "We miss the Graffiti Man down here, and the boys love those kinky jelly sweets you bring with you. They ain't affordable for the likes of us but you being the man and all, we figure you have some dosh to give us a treat now and then."

Kinky jelly sweets? Clay stared at Tate, whose face had taken on a flush, and he was doing a good job of not looking at Clay.

"Yeah, I'll bring some next time I'm down. It's not like I have a secret stash anywhere, you know? Anyway, we need to get on so see you guys later, yeah?"

Tate did the complicated handshake again and then sauntered off down the alley. Oh no, you don't, Clay thought as he walked faster to catch Tate up. That bit of information is too delicious not to interrogate you about.

"So, kinky jelly sweets?" Clay murmured as he lightly grabbed Tate's arm to slow him down to talk. "Want to tell me about that?"

"It's nothing," Tate muttered sulkily. "How come I knew you'd fixate on that fact?"

Clay gave an amused snort. "I hardly think asking my fiancé about jelly sweets once is a fixation," he remarked drily. "I am intrigued though. Have you been into Dare's shop BonBon Bizarre or Lewd Foods, buying up jelly penises perhaps?"

From the scowl Tate gave Clay was sure he'd guessed right. He let out a loud guffaw, causing a couple to turn around and stare at them curiously. "I'm right, aren't I? You kinky devil. What else have you got hidden in a goodie bag at home?"

"Nothing that concerns you," Tate snorted, his tone amused. "Let a man have some fucking secrets, won't you?"

Clay nodded sagely. "Chocolate dildo, edible underwear, 'eat me out' lube? When was I going to enjoy the fruits of your labour? You've tasted mine."

"The way you're carrying on, never," Tate hissed as he cast Clay a dark glance. "Now could you stop talking about it in public? You'll make people think we're a pair of perverts."

Clay sidled closer. "Nothing perverted about me spreading you open and enjoying a little strawberry delight while I'm down there," he murmured softly. He grinned when Tate hitched a breath and his hand drifted down to his groin. "You like that idea, don't you, babe?"

"Jesus, Clay," Tate said huskily. "You really want to do this now, out here?" He waved a hand as they passed the sweets shop in question. Lewd Foods was filled with a number of people in the popular shop. The thought of Tate being one of those people, buying sexy goodies that they could both enjoy turned Clay on and his cock was making itself known.

Tate walked faster, striding ahead of Clay who ambled behind with a grin. God, I love making him hot and bothered. Bodes well for tonight.

Clay couldn't wait to get home.

Chapter 9

Something told Tate it would be a long fucking day. Not only had he woken up with a throat that was scratchy and sore from snoring, no doubt thanks to the whisky he'd drunk a little too much of last night. He absolutely didn't need the disaster Archie had left – he'd crapped all over the kitchen floor.

Clay had left early this morning in a taxi for a 4 a.m. flight to Stuttgart to work a case. Tate swore unhappily knowing Archie had waited until after Clay had gone to leave Tate a waking up present. There was no way Clay wouldn't have cleaned up had he seen it.

Sighing, Tate staggered into the kitchen, clad in only a pair of boxers, and cleaned up, choking and controlling the urge to hurl as he did. He prided himself on his gag reflex, but this, this was torture. Fuck, the stench. What the hell has this pup eaten that his insides smell so dead?

Archie lay in the kitchen corner, head on his paws, large brown eyes gazing at Tate sorrowfully.

"You can look at me like that all you want," Tate muttered as he held his breath, making his way to the guest toilet in the hallway to flush the offending evidence. Archie trotted along behind him. "Bad dog." Tate scolded. "You're supposed to come tell me when you want to go out, remember?"

Archie whined pathetically and Tate narrowed his eyes. "Don't play that cute puppy card with me, buster. Clay may not be able to resist, but you've got me now. The big bad daddy."

He hid a grin as Archie huffed and rolled over onto his belly, inviting a scratch. Tate ignored him and walked back to the kitchen for the disinfectant spray and the mop. He cleaned up thoroughly, sprayed more disinfectant in the air to be safe, then took a well-earned shower. Half an hour later, feeling like a new man and dressed in a comfortable sweatshirt and pants, Tate was ready to catch up with the world and see if anything new had happened on

Olivia's case. It had been two days since they'd visited Joshua and neither they nor the police had made any more headway into finding the woman.

Tate wasn't a pessimist, but he feared the worst. Statistics weren't on their side. After the first 72 hours, most kidnapping victims were found dead. He scanned once again through the file they had containing photos, notes, eyewitness accounts and some useful documents Rick had sent over. Nothing stood out.

"No fucking clue where you are, Olivia," Tate muttered as he leaned back in his chair and rubbed his eyes tiredly. "This is one fuck-up of a mystery."

His mobile rang, and Tate frowned when he saw the caller's name. "Tomas? I thought you were in Lithuania? Everything okay?"

"Yes, all is fine." Tomas's voice echoed down the phone hollowly as if he was in a large room and the sound seemed to bounce off the walls. "I am still in Lithuania and I am calling to tell you I spoke with Tanvi this morning at the same time she received another mould of chocolate from the kidnapper. Has she called you yet?"

Tate shook his head. "Not yet. I'll call her once I'm finished with you. Do you know if she's called the police? You know, the cops who are assigned to this case?"

There was silence. "I am not sure," Tomas admitted. "Relio might have contacted them, I suppose. She said she would call him too after we spoke." His tone was non-committal and Tate sensed something not right.

"You suppose? You and Relio are tight as a nun's butt-cheeks, you know everything that happens. Did you ask him?"

"Relio and I are not talking to each other at this moment," Tomas declared, somewhat haughtily. "He is being childish and I have no time to deal with it."

Tate snorted. "Honeymoon over, then? I'm not even going to ask you what the issue was because you guys are both damned divas. For all I know, it could have been an argument over who likes Marmite and who doesn't."

There was another silence on the other end of the phone. "People argue over something like that?" Tomas said, sounding confused. "I detest it and Relio knows this. He will never serve me toast with that foul stuff, so how could we argue over it?"

Tate closed his eyes and took a deep, calming breath. "It was rhetorical. I didn't really expect an answer. Shit. Never mind. I'll give Rick a call then, ask him to send someone around to pick up the mould thingy for his forensics team."

"Call Tanvi first, please, and let her know when you will go visit her?" Tomas huffed into the phone. "She sounded quite upset on the phone."

Tate nodded. "I will. In fact, I'll shoot out now and see her. I'll call her on the way."

"Thank you, Tate." Tomas's tone softened. "As Relio is not talking to me, will you visit him too and tell him I said hello?"

"What the fuck, am I your messenger boy now?" Tate demanded. "Pick up the phone and tell him yourself."

"I tried to call him yesterday, and we ended up having a big argument. He is not answering my calls now." Tomas sighed. "He doesn't realise how much I owe to Valentin and how much he needs me right now. All Relio wants is for me to come home."

"Oh, for Christ's sake." Tate stood up and paced around the room. "Is Valentin the reason you left suddenly to go home? He a good friend of yours?"

All Tate heard was breathing until Tomas replied. "Yes," he said sadly. "Val is a dear friend, and he is suffering. I have to be here until it is over." Tate didn't want to pry further. He'd heard these sorts of conversations before. Hell, he'd even been involved in a couple. It sounded like whatever Valentin was going through, Tomas needed to help him through it. And as much as he wasn't really an Aurelio fan, Tate didn't think Tomas's compassion would upset the older man. Something else was going on.

"I'm really sorry to hear that," Tate said. "I'll go down to the club after seeing Tanvi and give Relio your message. But I draw the fucking line at hugging or kissing him for you. In fact, there can be no contact at all, *capisce*?"

"*Capisce*," Tomas agreed. "I would not want you to do either of those things so you are safe. Thank you, my friend." The line went dead.

Tate made sure Archie had food, that he'd had a toilet break out in the garden, because Tate wanted no more little packages to clean up when he got home.

Within a half hour of Tomas's call, Tate was wheeling the bike out for his journey.

***

When Tate reached Chocerotica and stepped inside, he was transported to a magical wonderland that looked as if Father Christmas had over decorated in a big way. Well, he mused as he sidestepped a large display of what looked like red and green foil-wrapped cocks set out like the fantail of a peacock, the season was only a month away. And he still had a fuck-ton of shopping to do. He had something special planned for Clay's gift. Something Tate had been working on for some time. He hoped Clay would like it.

Tate shuddered as he passed yet another homage to the crazy season in the form of large naked lady lollies dressed in sparkling sequin nipple caps and a strategically placed blob of silver tinsel over the privates. It wasn't that Tate was squeamish about seeing lady bits—after all when he'd been undercover in the drug squad, among some of the most homophobic people he'd ever known, he'd seen more than one real naked woman and her private parts. That was the nature of the job. He'd had lap dances from many, and more than once been invited into the private back room for a party. Sometimes, he'd accepted, under the watchful, steely gaze of Sonny Armerian, his then-lover, captor and tormentor. He had allowed Tate to make a show of liking women, but God help him if he ever did anything with them.

He shivered at the memory and tried to bring his head back into the present.

"Tate, I am so pleased to see you." Tanvi scurried up to him, her face pale and drawn, and she wrapped her arms around him. "Thanks for calling your nephew. The police are on their way over to fetch the letter and the mould. I put them in clear plastic bags, but I wanted you to see it first and to take pictures."

Tate gave the woman in his arms an awkward hug. "Yeah, sounds good. Let's look, see if anything strikes us as different. We need a fucking break on this one."

He followed Tanvi into the backroom and stopped short at what greeted him on her desk. "Wow. That's a little different to the last thing they sent."

It was surreal to see Olivia's face staring up at them beneath the plastic bag. The chocolate kidnapper had gone all out on this one, and Tate couldn't help feeling a chill down his spine as he remembered the death masks he'd seen once in a museum. He hoped like hell that wasn't the case now. He leaned over the creation, picking up the mould gingerly, and peering at it.

"This is an unusual way to communicate," he muttered as he turned the mask over. "I'm assuming they sent another letter with this one?"

Tanvi nodded and pointed toward a piece of cream-coloured notepaper on the desk, also encased in plastic. "They did, and it's much the same thing as the last one they sent." She managed a smile. "I touched it when I opened the envelope to read it, but the police have my fingerprints from last time so it should be okay. If there is anything new on them, they'll be able to discount mine."

Tate grinned. "You've been watching too much CSI." He frowned as he put the mask down and picked up the letter.

Once again it was typed. Plain, computer type, nothing special about it.

I am sending you this as more proof that Olivia is with me, and safe. I understand your concern about her welfare and there is no need to be worried. I am not a monster. I am her friend. I do not deserve to go to hell.

Tate blinked at that last statement. It seemed familiar but he couldn't remember where he'd heard it.

I am happy that the police are dealing with the problem, and as soon as I am sure it has been removed permanently, I will bring Olivia home.

That was it. Tate stared up at Tanvi. "Clay and I think the 'problem' they refer to is Olivia's boyfriend. This seems to confirm that theory since the police pulled him in again for an interview yesterday. But how does the kidnapper know that?"

Tanvi shrugged. "I understand they went to Allan's workplace to ask him to come in for questioning again as a 'person of interest.'" She chuckled at Tate's confounded expression. "I know that because Freddy told me. He and his graffiti friends are all-knowing, all-seeing in this neck of the woods. You know that."

Tate puffed out air and laughed softly. "Yeah, I do. So our kidnapper thinks the cops talking to Smith goes part way to solving the problem? It's only questioning, the guy hasn't done anything wrong that we know about. Until Olivia herself presses charges for any physical abuse she's suffered at his hands, nothing will change." He scowled. "Our kidnapper might be clever, but they aren't clued in on how it all works in the real world. It's like they've got this romantic vision of rescuing the damsel in distress, and everything will magically fix itself into a happy ever after."

Tanvi went over to the small kitchen workstation at the back of her office and began filling up the water tank on the coffee machine. "The good news is that it doesn't sound as if this person has any intention to harm her. That's comforting."

She busied herself setting up the machine. Soon the fresh and welcome smell of roasted coffee wafted through the air and tickled Tate's nostrils.

He took photos of the mask from different angles, as well as he could through the shiny plastic, and of the letter, and finally the plain cardboard box the items had been in.

"They could have left this on the doorstep," Tate mused as he moved around the table. "Instead, they're posting it which means they understand the CCTV cameras in the area are a danger." He tucked his phone back into his pocket. "I'll load all the images when I get home, give them another once over."

"Did Allan have anything further to say once the police had spoken to him?" Tanvi asked worriedly.

"Nothing new," Tate grumbled. "He said the same stuff as before. He doesn't know where Olivia is, he never hurt her." He scoffed, "It's the usual thing of a suspect saying they're as innocent as virgin snow. The thing is, from what the police gathered from the neighbours and friends, there's no evidence anywhere to substantiate any physical abuse claims. They all say Allan was a nasty bit of work and was a real tosser for putting Olivia down and bossing her around, but they saw nothing physical."

"But that happens a lot, doesn't it?" Tanvi asked. "People can hide the bruises and cuts. And abusers know where to hurt people so it doesn't show."

Tate nodded thoughtfully. It sounded as if Tanvi had some personal experience with this. "That's true," he acknowledged. "And we won't ignore that fact. When we find Olivia, she'll need to give us the truth. The kidnapper has said nowhere there was anything physical. They may have taken exception to the way Allan talked to Olivia or treated her in public. Perhaps that's the only place he or she could have seen it happen." He looked down at the letter. "If Allan is the problem this person is trying to solve, then they reduce him to an 'it,' not making it personal, making it distant and like a nasty smell that needs removing from Olivia's life."

They were both quiet for a while, contemplating the items laid out on the desk. A shout from the front of the shop startled both. "Hello? Ms Sharma, it's DS Meadham here with the forensics team."

Tanvi shot out to the front of the shop. "Good afternoon, Detective Sergeant." There was the sound of greeting and curt orders being given and Tate smiled at Carol Meadham when she entered the room. "It wasn't me, I swear," he joked with his hands in the air. "It's good to see you."

Carol grinned at him. "You too. We meet again in less than savoury circumstances." She eyed the plastic-bagged items on the table. "I doubt we'll get much from these but we'll try it. The forensic team are dusting outside, on the sill and door, in case the kidnapper touched it. It'll be a headache to discount all the fingerprints from the shoppers but at least we'll have a database to match against if we get a proper print if our perpetrator slipped up." She sighed heavily. "That poor girl. We're doing everything we can to find her but there are no fresh leads. All we can do is keep trying and hope we catch a break soon."

Tanvi entered the room, and they watched as Carol collected the items and put them into another large plastic bag with a red rim, sealed it and filled in the lines with black magic marker. "There. I'll send this onto the lab when I get back to the station, but it will take a while. There's a backlog and unfortunately, we have to wait in line like everyone else."

"I appreciate everything you and Tate are doing to find Olivia," Tanvi said. "Strangely enough, I trust whoever has her when he or she says Olivia is safe. I don't think this person would harm her."

Tate's mobile phone rang, and he left Tanvi and Carol chatting. *Clay.* "Hey, babe," Tate murmured as he found a quiet place to talk in the corner of the shop. "How's Stuttgart?"

"Fucking cold, filled with obstinate, pig-headed people who won't listen to sense, and did I mention fucking cold?" Clay laughed as someone swore at him in German. "Anton says hello."

Tate laughed. Anton Fischer was a part of Clay's team in Germany and no doubt the stubborn, obstinate part of Clay's description. The two men had a history spanning back to their time in the military. "Sounds as if you're doing well, then. Tell him I say hi back. How is the meeting going?"

"As good as expected. The client has finally agreed to appoint a new security firm because, hello, the last one was fucking stealing from him, and I'm confident Anton will carry on with the identify fraud investigation with at least some reliable cover behind him." Clay was fiercely protective of his operatives and having a client who didn't see things the same way he did, would not have gone down well. "Anyway, I'm hoping to be on a plane back home around six pm. I won't be staying over."

"Sounds good. Archie misses you. Plus, he crapped all over the floor this morning after you left. I think he did it on purpose."

Clay's sputter of laughter warmed Tate's soul. "Oh Christ, I know what you're like when you smell shit and vomit. I wish I'd been a fly on the wall."

Tate chuckled wryly. "Trust me. It wasn't a pretty sight. I'm glad you're coming home. I have a few updates of my own to share. You'll be home about what, nine pm?"

"Yeah, about that as long as the flights are on time." Clay's tone softened. "Excellent, I look forward to a catch-up with you. Give Archie a kiss from me, will you, and tell him I'll see him later."

"Will do. Safe flight home." Tate disconnected the call and looked over at Tanvi and DS Meadham who were still talking. "I'll be off. Back to work. Carol, can I ask that when your lab get the plastic off the evidence, they send me the photos they take too, so I can add them to our case file?"

Carol nodded. "Sure, Tate. I don't know how long that will be."

He shrugged. "No worries, I have some images to keep me going. Not that I think they'll give us much, but you never know." He inclined his head at the two women. "See you soon, and if I hear anything new, you'll be the first to know."

He waved goodbye and stepped out of the shop. He'd go pass on Tomas's message to Aurelio and give the man an update at the same time, then he'd head home. He had chicken to cook for dinner, a minibar to restock and he also wanted to make sure he was properly prepared.

Tonight Tate wanted to welcome his man home in style.

Chapter 10

Clay let himself into the house, dumped his cabin bag onto the hall floor and sighed in relief. It had been a good journey home, but the day had been long. He was looking forward to having something to eat, saying hello to Tate and Archie, and then sitting down and having a drink.

"I'm home," he called out, wondering where the excited puppy greeting was. Usually, Archie came bouncing to whoever got in the door first, and the pup had been known to piddle in excitement. Clay had had to clean more than one pair of shoes since they'd got the mutt. "Tate, you here?" He removed his jacket, laid it over the chair and went to look for his fiancé.

"In here," Tate called out. The voice came from the kitchen and Clay pushed the door open to be greeted by the sight of his lover bending over the sink, washing a dish. What stopped him short, though, was the sight of Tate's firm, high arse cheeks clad in nothing but a pair of black open-back leather briefs which bared not only both of his delectable cheeks but the dragon tattoo on his right one. Even though the tattoo-covered a scar that Tate would prefer to forget, Clay couldn't deny it was as sexy as fuck.

Jesus, since when did he start wearing those? Clay could hardly form a coherent thought as he ogled Tate's backside.

"Won't be a minute," Tate said. He turned to grin at Clay and there was a definite wicked sparkle in his eyes. "I just got out of the shower and started preparing dinner. Did you have a good flight home?" He turned back to his plate washing.

"Fuck the flight home," Clay managed huskily. "Jesus, what a sight to greet a man. That bit of nothing another purchase from Fet for Life?" Lately, Tate had bought an occasional item from the fetish wear shop and was now the proud owner of a chest harness and a leather jockstrap. He'd bought Clay a pair of front zip-up wet look boxers and they'd enjoyed more than one night of pleasure with them.

Tate put the plate in the dish rack and turned around with a smirk. Clay swallowed when he saw that Tate's apparel also had a zip upfront. His man was surely in a mood to play tonight. Beneath his suit pants, Clay was hard, his cock pushing tantalisingly against the fabric.

"Cat got your tongue?" Tate murmured. His gaze darted down toward Clay's groin. "From the look of Clayzilla, I'm guessing you like this look." Clay didn't even argue with him about the use of the pet name Tate had given his dick.

"Oh, my tongue is peachy," Clay shot back with a smile he knew Tate would recognise. Judging from the hungry expression on Tate's face, Clay was sure his intentions to debauch him had been understood. "And I intend putting it to good use. Turn around over the sink again."

Tate's eyes darkened and his tongue came out to lick his lips, leaving them wet and shining. Then he turned around and placed his hands above the sink, leaning his body in and arching his back out so his arse was ripe for the taking.

Clay knelt behind him, his hands caressing the smooth skin of Tate's arse. "God, look at you," Clay muttered. "So damned gorgeous and all mine." His lips took the place of his hands as he trailed them over Tate's pebbled skin. Goosebumps had formed and Clay licked at them. "I'm going to open you up and show you exactly what my tongue can do."

Tate shuddered, and his body tensed as Clay prised open his cheeks. It was a little more difficult than usual given the underwear, but he got a good grip and exposed Tate's hole. "So beautiful," Clay whispered and wiggled the tip of his tongue into Tate's opening. He tasted of soap and citrus and Clay inhaled deeply, loving his man's scent. Tate's breathing deepened and Clay began his assault.

"Oh fuck," Tate groaned, his arse pushing back into Clay's face. "I love the feel of your mouth on me." His hand left the wall, and he fumbled at the zipper of his underwear. "I need to touch myself, Clay, You're driving me crazy."

Clay stopped his lavish worship of Tate's hole and grinned. "You touch that zipper and I stop. That cock is mine to play with. Be patient, babe. I'll get to it."

He ignored Tate's expletives as he went back to what he was doing. His own cock was begging to be let out and touched, but this game was fun and both of them could wait a little longer.

When Tate's legs trembled, and he began knocking his forehead against the wall in frustration, Clay took pity on him. To be fair, he was in dire need of needing to be manhandled too so there was an element of selfishness in his decision to stop.

He stood up, pulled Tate around to face him then took his mouth in a blistering kiss that went straight down to his soul and flared into his chest with the warmth of a thousand suns. Kissing Tate was his favourite thing to do. His man held nothing back, he was rough, passionate and often brutal. Clay loved it.

Clay pulled away, and both men stared at each other, chests heaving. "I want to unzip you so you can fuck my mouth but I don't want to catch your skin," Clay panted out. "Remember last time? I'd hate a repeat."

Tate's pupils were blown, and dazed, his lips swollen. He nodded and closed his eyes as Clay gingerly unzipped him, taking care not to catch Tate's cock or any other sensitive bits. The "last time" he'd referred to had been when the two of them had got rough when Clay had his pair of zip-up boxers on, and the pain Clay had felt when his dick got caught had been agonising.

Tate's cock sprung out, and Clay groaned in appreciation at the sight. He wasted no time, and took it in his mouth, cheeks hollowing and throat clenching as he pleasured the man above who was making the sexiest and dirtiest noises.

"Jesus, baby, it won't take long," Tate managed between gritted teeth as he drove his cock into Clay's mouth deeper. "That rim job you gave me was epic. I'm surprised I didn't come in my underwear."

Clay took that as a sign that he was doing a good job and continued to up his game. He could tell when Tate was near release as he had a habit of making a strange, surprised "oh" when his orgasm triggered. After a few more deep pulls, come flooded into Clay's mouth, the taste familiar and welcome.

Tate gripped his head hard, his body wracked with shudders. "Fuck," he gasped. "Oh my God."

Clay drew back, Tate's slick cock popping from his mouth. "Now that's what I call a welcome home present," he said in satisfaction, his jaw aching. Clay loved giving head.

He stood, trying not to wince too much as his knees creaked a little. He hoped Tate hadn't heard it. He'd never live it down. Clay lowered his trousers and underwear and pressed his dick into Tate's already searching hand. "Now jack me off," he commanded. "That way I can kiss you at the same time."

Tate's lips found his while his fingers wrapped around Clay's aching cock. It didn't take long before Clay was shouting his release into Tate's mouth and they were both plastered against each other covered in sweat. Tate's tight undies were near painted on his hips, his half-hard cock wet and slick against his body. "Jesus," he groaned softly. "These things are restricting my circulation. I need to get them off." He fumbled with them, swearing as they refused to peel off easily, clinging to his sweat-soaked skin.

Clay pulled out a kitchen stool and sat down, satiated and feeling rather pleased with himself. "You knew wearing those damn things," he gestured to the briefs, "would make me horny so you deserved everything you got." He smirked. "Good luck getting out of them."

He chuckled in amusement as Tate's expletives got even dirtier, and the contortions of his fiancé's body as he finally got rid of the underwear gave Clay some rather naughty ideas.

"I knew you were flexible, but wow, some of those moves you had going there were interesting," he murmured as Tate gave a heartfelt sigh of relief.

"Yeah? Well, take a picture, it'll last longer," Tate muttered, reaching over and picking up a bunch of wet wipes from the cupboard. He got to work wiping some mess off his body then handed some fresh ones to Clay. "I'm not feeling like a shower again right now so this will have to do." He grinned wryly. "I confess my plan was to have dinner first, watch you get all hot and bothered while we ate, then take you to bed and ream your arse. Then return the favour. I didn't count on a rim job right in the middle of the kitchen. I'm sure that went against health and safety rules." His husky laugh made Clay think more dirty thoughts.

"Fuck health and safety," Clay said laconically. "Your arse, those shorts, they were made for immediate action." He reached out and trailed his fingers down Tate's stomach, which smelt pleasantly of lemon from the wipes. "So, is there still food to eat?" he asked hopefully. "I could do with something. Someone made me hungry."

Tate sighed. "Yeah, Mr Romantic, I made Selina Chicken. All it'll take is warming up and boiling some rice."

Clay leaned over and kissed Tate. "Wine, your dish of the day, and you. Sounds like the perfect ending to the day." He stood up. "Seeing as how I didn't even get undressed out of my suit, let me change into something more comfortable then I'll be with you." He frowned. "Where's Archie? I haven't seen him since I came home."

Tate sauntered over to the dryer and pulled out a pair of sweatpants. He was all toned limbs and tight muscles and Clay heaved a sigh of appreciation at the sight. "Archie is next door," Tate smiled. "You know that June's kid had an operation last week?" He pulled on a pair of sweatpants that hung low on his hips, leaving the sexy V of his torso exposed.

Clay nodded. Their neighbour, June Osmond, was a single mom living with a ten-year-old who'd unfortunately succumbed to appendicitis recently.

"Well, seems Riley was being a bit of a pain in the arse about being bed-bound and hasn't been sleeping well. I saw June in her garden this afternoon when I was walking Archie. I know Riley loves Arch, and he loves the kid, so I offered to loan the pup tonight. Maybe that'll cheer the kid up and give June a break." He snorted. "The woman has bags under her eyes Gucci would be proud of."

"Aww, how sweet," Clay teased, his chest secretly full at the thought of Tate helping their neighbour like that. "Careful. You'll give the impression you're not as tough as you look."

Tate gave him the finger. "Their mistake." He grinned. "Archie was thrilled to be over there, and last time I saw him he was wearing a baseball cap and Riley was taking his picture for Instacrap or whatever that thing is called."

Clay rolled his eyes. "Instagram, you heathen." Tate didn't do social media.

"Whatever. We can pick him up in the morning and take him for a walk before work." He took a creased cut off tee-shirt from the dryer and shrugged into it. "Right, I'll heat up dinner and put the rice on." Tate gave a soft laugh. "Tuck your cock back in or get changed before I dish up."

Clay took the hint and went into the bedroom to change. When he came out clad in a comfy pair of jogging pants and a polo shirt, Tate sat at the kitchen island. Two plates of something delicious smelling sat on the tabletop and he'd already poured the wine. The fragrance of garlic bread wafted through the kitchen and Clay's mouth filled with saliva. He was bloody starving.

As they ate, Tate told Clay the latest new about Olivia's disappearance and the delivery of the new chocolate mould. "I've got this new imaging computer programme Draven recommended," Tate remarked as he munched on another piece of bread. "He swears it's magic and the only thing to use when you want to run image results side by side and compare. I thought I'd combine all the crime scene photos we have together in this programme and see if anything jumps out." He shrugged. "It's worth a try. We might have missed something."

Draven Samuels was one of Clay's top operatives, if not the best. Unlike Tate, he was a lover of the latest IT and technology gadgets and Tate took Draven's recommendations seriously. Clay grinned inwardly. His two Alpha male colleagues colluding together was always a sight to see. The testosterone factor was strong in them, he thought in a Yoda parody.

"Sounds like a plan." He mopped up the last of his chicken sauce with his piece of bread and consumed it. "That was delicious, babe. My turn to cook tomorrow night." Clay stood up and collected the dirty dishes. He started packing them in the dishwasher as Tate busied himself wiping down the counter and the stove.

Once kitchen duty was over, Clay took their wine glasses through to the lounge and sat down on the couch. Time for a little R and R, he thought as Tate settled in beside him and picked up the remote.

The pup is on holiday, my belly is full and my man is beside me. What else could a man want?

***

The following morning Clay went to collect Archie from the neighbour while Tate snored loudly in bed. His fiancé had had a rough night, tossing and turning and mumbling in his sleep. Clay wasn't sure what was keeping him awake, but occasionally Tate's nightmares came back to haunt him. There had been nothing to trigger them, and Clay hoped it was merely an anomaly. Tate's brain often worked in strange ways.

Clay walked Archie down the tree-lined streets of their neighbourhood, bought groceries from the fruit and veg stall—some broccoli and courgettes he fancied for dinner with the steak dish he was cooking tonight—and purchased a tasty pig's ear for Archie to gnaw on when he got home. It would keep the pup quiet while he and Tate worked on the case. Finally, they were both settled in the study, steaming cups of coffee next to them, along with two Belgian Buns Clay had treated them to.

"Let's look at you," Tate muttered as he pulled up the file of images. "I got all the police images from Rick's team, along with the ones Tanvi and I took. It's a lot to go through but hell, we have got nothing else to work with."

It was a time-consuming process, and they took it in turns to get the pictures up and then scrutinise them, enlarge them and agree on what they were seeing.

Clay stood up, stretched as he contemplated putting eye drops into his tired eyes. As he moved to do so, Tate stiffened and leaned in intently. The screen reflected different shots of the chocolate moulds from all angles.

"Look at that." Tate enlarged the picture of Olivia's ear mould, watching as the image became clearer. Clay moved closer and peered at the screen. "Do you see something there, on the right-hand side?" he asked excitedly. "I wasn't sure whether it was some drip or flaw in the mould, but now I look closer, it looks like something else. Here, look."

Clay squinted at the area Tate showed. "At first glance, it looks like nothing, but when you focus…" His eyes widened. "It could be letters."

Tate nodded grimly. "I make out a J and an O. What do you see?"

"I think it's a J and an N." Clay frowned in thought. "What could it be? Something used in the mould making process, some sort of trademark perhaps on the rubber mould?"

Tate shook his head. "I have no idea. Perhaps it's something, perhaps nothing."

"Bring up the face mould," Clay said, sitting back down, a little more energised now something might be happening. "Let's see if the other mould has any weird markings the same as the ear."

Tate clicked several buttons and the images on the screen enlarged, featuring nothing but the various pictures of the chocolate face shot from varying angles. They studied the images and after a few minutes, Tate sighed and sat back, rubbing his eyes. "I think my brain has gone to sleep," he grumbled. "I'm not seeing anything, are you?"

Clay reached over and enlarged the picture a little more, swearing as the pixels blurred. "I thought I saw something there." He pointed with his finger toward the inside of the mould, at chin level. "Doesn't that look like letters to you?"

Tate squinted, turning his head once side to the other. "Let me try to clear the image up more. I don't think I can do much more with it, but let's try one more time."

Once again he clicked a few keys and slowly, before Clay's eyes, the image became clearer.

Tate slapped the desk in jubilation. "Jesus, more letters," he said excitedly. "I think it's another J and an O, maybe followed by an S?"

Clay narrowed his eyes to focus on the tiny imperfections in the chocolate. "I agree with you," he said finally, excitement coursing through his veins. "J, O and S. That can only be one person, surely?"

"Joshua," they said together and stared at one another in both disbelief and hope.

"You think Olivia has been carving in letters to tell us who has her?" Tate stood up and strode around the study. "It's so faint, she must have used a pin or something to make them. She probably didn't have enough time to complete the name or got interrupted perhaps, but this time she at least managed another letter."

"It's a lead," Clay agreed. "The question is, do we tell Rick about this or do we stake Joshua out first, see if this goes anywhere?"

Tate shook his head fiercely. "It's a tenuous link, and we need to be sure. I say let's find out where Joshua lives, look around. If we find anything concrete, then we call in the cops. They can take it from there." His eyes glinted with excitement. "We have a fucking lead," he said. "Fucking finally." He looked down at his watch, a chunky Globenfeld Sports model Clay had bought Tate for his last birthday. "We can go now and scope his place out."

"Best give Tomas a call then, see if he can get us the address. Hazel told us Joshua is living in a basement flat in Shepard's Bush, so that narrows things down right away." Clay gave a wry smile. "If anyone can tell us his address, he can."

Tate picked up his phone and punched out a number. Clay went back to searching the screen for any more information. The more he looked at the pictures, the more he thought they were on the right track. There definitely appeared to be letters carved into the chocolate. Letters that wouldn't be there naturally given what they were. Tate disappeared out into the garden as he spoke animatedly to Tomas. Clay got up to make them another cup of coffee, turning when Tate strode back into the room.

"Tomas will do a bit of digging and get us an address," Tate said in satisfaction. "I'm sure it won't take too long."

Tate was right. Within less than five minutes, Tomas had called them back with an address.

"His basement flat in Shepherd's Bush is part of a commercial property," Tomas explained. He didn't sound like his usual bouncy self. "It looks like owners rent the flat to Joshua for a small amount. The business property is empty and boarded up. From what I can see, it's private and out of the way." There was the sound of clicking. "I've sent the images to your phone, Tate, plus the address. Do you really think it is this Joshua that has Livvy?"

Tate's phone beeped, and he peered at the images Tomas had sent through, Clay looking over his shoulder. "It's a possibility," he agreed. The building was in a small commercial area with shop fronts and narrow, dark alleyways. "We'll check this out. When are you back in the country? How is your friend doing?"

There was silence from the other end of the phone. When Tomas spoke, he sounded tired and sad. "I think I will be home soon," he said quietly. "Valentin passed away yesterday morning. I am staying to sort out his funeral for his family and then I will be back."

"God, Tomas, I'm so sorry about your loss," Clay said, his heart aching at the sadness in Tomas's tone. "That sucks. Let us know if we can do anything for you." He cleared his throat. Hopefully, my question won't upset him. "Have you spoken to Relio? Told him?"

Tomas sighed. "I have. I needed him last night." He snorted. "Even though he makes me mad."

Clay smiled as he imagined the scowl on Tomas's face. He was glad the two men were talking though. Relio had been a bear with a sore head the last week.

"I'm pleased you two are speaking. He might not let you know it, but he misses you. Don't tell him I told you that, though."

"Really? He said that?" Tomas suddenly sounded lighter. "He's an ass. He never tells me these things. I have to detect them."

Tate sniggered next to Clay. "Men are arseholes, Tomas. You should know that by now." He cast a fond glance at Clay.

"I am aware," Tomas muttered. "Anyway, I need to go. Let me know what happens with your mission, I am waiting in eagerness." He rang off and Tate laughed out loud.

"That young man and his strange phrases. Sounds like he and Aurelio are working things out, though."

Clay nodded. "About time. Relio was becoming a pain in the arse."

At Tate's raised eyebrow, Clay chuckled. "Not in that way, you idiot. I only let you debauch me that way." He walked over to pick up his jacket from the coat rack. "Come on, let's go do a little surveillance work. I know how much you love that."

"Fuck surveillance," Tate muttered. "Last time I did that, a house blew up on me. I'm taking my lock picks with me and getting up close and personal with this guy's place."

"You know that's illegal," Clay murmured as they walked out the door toward the driveway where the bike was parked. It was a cool afternoon, and the bike would do. "I'm not sure I can condone that, being your partner and all."

Tate grinned at him. "Pot calling the kettle black, babe." He shrugged into his leather jacket and took his helmet from the bike panier. "I seem to remember a certain someone who blackmailed a local councilman into letting us rummage around in the council files in the middle of the night, looking for land records to prove a crime."

Clay pursed his lips as he climbed onto the bike, Tate settling behind him. "The bloody idiot should have kept his love of gambling and prostitutes a better secret then. Besides, those land records were the only thing standing between us and that dick of a landlord who ran that exotic animal smuggling ring." He pulled on his helmet and started the bike. "Sometimes, the end justifies the means."

He roared off into the street, Tate hugging him tightly.

God, I hope this lead pans out.

Chapter 11

"Christ, how the fuck can it grow so cold, like within an hour?" Tate pulled his jacket tighter around him. "It looks like it will snow."

I hate being on the bike when it fucking snows.

Clay glanced at him with amusement. Tate knew he'd worn a perpetual scowl ever since they'd climbed off the bike half an hour ago.

I fucking hate the cold. If a man was meant to be out in these temperatures, I'd sprout bloody wings and be called Penguin.

"Stop being such a pussy," Clay remarked as he sipped his takeaway coffee. "I want to get the lay of the land before we go in there." He gestured toward Joshua's flat. They'd been standing around observing the place, familiarising themselves with the neighbourhood activities. It was a busy little street, more so than Tate had imagined.

He muttered under his breath, casting a dark look at Clay, who, as usual ignored it. He motioned with his head to something taking place on the corner. "That guy over there is blatantly selling something he shouldn't be. He's had a queue of visitors talking to him since we got here. Might be worth mentioning it to Rick."

"There's always something happening on street corners," Tate grumbled. "It's like a rite of passage for them." He flicked a finger over at the opposite side of the road. "Looks like that pawn shop is a front for something. There's been more traffic into that place of business than there are bacon sarnies in the breakfast caff over there." He glanced longingly at the café. "Speaking of which…"

Clay nudged him. "I promise I'll buy you the biggest breakfast sandwich you can eat after we finish here. Come on, let's go see whether we can break into Joshua's place without getting caught." Clay had already called Chocolate Heaven and verified he was at work today, and wasn't due home for hours.

Joshua's place was a small, empty and boarded up shop, bearing the legend "Beatbuster Video" on the grimy glass window. Beside the shop was a set of stone stairs with iron railings along the walkway leading down into a basement section under the shop floor. Over the railings numerous baskets were draped, all sporting a myriad of flowers and colour. It was like a bright, tropical jungle oasis. The dwelling sported large, green plants in the bay window. It was private and given where it was situated, if Olivia was in there, no one would be any the wiser. Given the commercial aspect of the neighbourhood, it was a well-maintained area. Outside the front door, there was a large pot plant holder, out of which bright pink geraniums grew.

Somebody loves flowers and plants Tate thought as he and Clay meandered over the road to the flat. Given the pedestrians and the pavement traffic, if they could sneak down there without incident, no one would give them a second glance.

Given what Tanvi had told them before about Joshua being not fond of people, Clay hoped no eagle-eyed and nosey neighbours saw anything they were doing. The two of them blended in first, loitering on the pavement, looking in shops and keeping an eagle eye out for anyone else that might have access to the flat.

"Come on," Tate muttered as he whipped onto the top step and made his way down. "I think we're safe enough now." Clay followed him down and together they stood at the entrance, a sturdy, solid oak door.

Tate took out his little set of tools. "Nothing fancy to get open," he said as he toggled his pick in the lock. "It should only take me a minute, even less. Ah, there we go," he pronounced in satisfaction. He slid inside, Clay close behind him. He pushed the door shut and together they waited with bated breath in case there was any commotion outside.

After a minute, they nodded at each other and began looking around Joshua's residence. They'd walked directly into the lounge, a deceivingly large room given the outer view. It was immaculate. Nothing looked out of place, and there was minimal decoration.

The walls bore no pictures and were a soft cream colour, even the inner door leading to what Tate imagined was a kitchen or hallway sporting the same shade. The furniture was grey, two large bean-bags set an equal distance apart, facing the wall-mounted television, connected to a variety of devices. A small side table sat perfectly centred between the two chairs. Other than that, there was nothing. No knick-knacks, no sideboard, nothing to tell you who lived there or who they were.

"Wow," he said, wide-eyed. "This takes minimalism to a whole new level." He opened the closed door and whistled as he stepped into the next room. "Check this out."

Clay followed Tate through, and they stood stock still. It was a kitchen, but like nothing he'd seen before. The kitchen was filled with nothing but cream gadgets, all the same model from the look of them and all gleaming. Again, the design was minimalist. There were no cutlery racks, or crafty holders carrying spatulas and whisks. Nothing marred the pale surface of the worktops and even the stove was colour coordinated along with the appliances. It looked like something out of a show home, although in Tate's opinion, personal touches sold the home. Not this clinical and monotone look that seemed almost science fiction in appearance. He reached down and brushed his finger over the counter-tops. They came away clean.

"Well, we already know Joshua is an introvert and," Clay waved a hand, "I guess this is his idea of tranquillity. See how it's all smooth, no patterns, even on the floor? Who can tell what goes on in someone else's mind? I like the look myself. We could take a leaf out of Joshua's décor book, rather than having everything splayed around as we do."

Tate grunted. "Good luck with that. We both have too much crap between us for this Feng Shui stuff."

There was another closed door beside the dishwasher. Clay opened it and revealed a wide hallway. Two rooms led off it. One was a bedroom, no doubt Joshua's, and the other was a bathroom. At the end, the passage turned left.

Tate thought it was time to make their presence known. "Hello?" he called out. "Is anyone here? Olivia, are you here?"

They paused their search to listen but there was nothing. Tate's stomach sank. Had they made a wrong call and Joshua had nothing to do with Olivia's disappearance? Was Olivia in another building somewhere else in the city?

Further down the hallway, Clay paused. "Do you hear that?" He cocked his head. "I thought I heard a voice." He stopped and listened. It came from around the corner of the hallway. Both men looked at each other.

"This is the weirdest laid out place I've ever seen," Tate murmured. "Who knew it had so much space down here?" He paced down the rest of the hallway, stopping when he got to the end and looking left. He turned to Clay, his chest fizzy with anticipation. "There's another room here," he whispered. "And there is definitely sound coming from it."

Both men approached the door with care, and Tate gave a low whistle. "That's no regular interior door lock," he said. "It's a Yale lock, usually used on exterior doors." He tested the door. It was locked.

Clay lifted an eyebrow. "But you can still pick it, can't you?"

Tate grinned. "There isn't a lock I can't pick with a little practice. But first..." He knocked rapidly on the door. "Hello? Anyone in there?"

There was a flurry of noise behind the door and a woman's excited voice echoed through the door. "Oh my God, is someone there? Please let me out. Please."

"Is that you, Olivia?" Clay asked as Tate got to work. He and Tate grinned like fools at each other.

We've found her.

"Yes, it's Olivia du Preez here. Oh my God, how did you find me? Was it the chocolate masks? Did it work?" She sounded in tears. Tate didn't blame the poor woman.

"Hold on, Olivia, I'm nearly there," he called out as he narrowed his eyes to focus and wielded his pick. "We'll tell you all about it when we get you out of there."

Finally, the door swung open and a petite, strawberry blonde barrelled out of the room and rushed into Clay's arms as if she was drowning in floodwaters and he was a lifeboat. "Thank you for finding me. I can't believe it, it's been so long, I thought I'd be here forever." She burst into tears and Clay held her close.

"It's okay, we've got you. You've caused quite a ruckus. Everyone was worried about you."

Tate pocketed his lock picks and went into the room Olivia had been in while Clay consoled her. The room was small and a little claustrophobic. It was pretty, pink and feminine and had a small television on the white dresser. It was a room designed by someone who'd seen a home decor magazine somewhere and thought this was the ideal room for a female. It was almost childish, what with a variety of teddy bears and a stuffed camel lolling at the bottom of the bed. Tate noticed with compassion that some of them seemed to have been cuddled, given the look of them. No doubt they'd been the only company Olivia had had.

There was a small fridge in the corner, with a kettle and a shelf filled with condiments, including tea and coffee. Tate opened the fridge to see all the staples: milk, butter, cream, cold drinks and a variety of cold meats and ready meals. No doubt for use in the microwave sitting incongruously on top of a wide, white chair next to the fridge. A small en suite bathroom offered a basin and a toilet.

Everything had been set up for Olivia to have food and liquids while Joshua was at work. That alone would prove pre-meditation on Joshua's part. A fact that might not do him any good in court.

It was all a little creepy and knowing someone had lived here for over two weeks, probably with no chance to leave the room, a shudder wracked Tate's body as the walls closed in on him. He remembered his own incarceration at the hands of a psycho that had not been half as comfortable as this. That had been more of a blood, chains and beating scenario, on a cold concrete floor, surrounded by his own piss and vomit.

For a minute, he was transported back to that time, his chest tightening and stomach roiling. He closed his eyes and took a few deep breaths, counting down from a hundred slowly until he felt more in balance. When he opened his eyes, Clay stood in front of him, his gaze concerned.

"Tate, you okay, baby? You've gone white as hell."

Tate drew another breath and tried to force a smile. "I'm good. Just a bit of history catching up with me."

Clay's warm hands squeezed Tate's shoulder. "Bad memories, huh?" He lifted one hand to caress Tate's cheek with calloused fingers. "Breathe, baby. I've got you."

Looking into Clay's beautiful green eyes always calmed Tate. The love, the tenderness and the deep understanding he saw in his lover's eyes was Tate's salvation. Clay had always been his rock.

He nodded his head. "I'm okay," he said huskily. "Let's get some pictures of this place and I guess I'd better give Rick a call."

He gave Clay a brief smile and pulled out his mobile. Rick's phone went to voicemail. Tate left a brief message telling him they'd found Olivia and could he send a car to collect her. He left out the bit about how they'd found her. He'd leave that to Rick to figure out. He always did.

Olivia sat shivering in the lounge, staring around with wide eyes. "He lives here?" she whispered. "It isn't friendly, is it?" She smiled shakily. "Joshua was good to me. He cares about me, that's why he did this." A look of panic crossed her face. "God, he won't go to prison, will he? I mean, I didn't ask to be here, but he only meant well."

"We can't say," Tate said grimly. "Did he abduct you from your home, or off the street or did you come to visit him?"

"I met him in the street as I was walking home from the film. He asked me if I'd like to visit him and have a drink." Olivia murmured. "I'm pretty sure he drugged and when I woke up, I was in that room." She shuddered. "He made me comfortable, and I didn't want for anything. He's sweet, really."

"Except for the fact he kept you here without your consent for over two weeks," Tate muttered. "It could have been a fancy place, but it was still a prison."

"Given what you said, the chances are he'll be charged with false imprisonment, not kidnapping," Clay said compassionately. "It'll all depend on what the Crown Prosecution Service—the CPS—charge him with. But let's not think about that now. We need to get you out of here and into police custody. Tate has asked them to send a car because I don't think we'd fit you on the motorbike." His chuckle seemed to put the young woman more at ease.

"How did you write those initials in the chocolate?" Tate asked curiously. "Without them, we'd still be in the dark. That was a great idea."

Olivia clutched a couch cushion close to her as if it were a treasured stuffed toy. "I could go to the main bathroom to shower, and I saw the chocolate moulds drying in the airing cupboard outside. I only had a few seconds to get a towel from the cupboard to take in and used a hairpin I found to make the letters. I didn't have long though. I didn't want him to see me."

"You're safe now," Clay said. "I'm sure the police will take care of Joshua and listen to what you say in his defence. Tell them everything you know and that might make things easier for him."

Olivia cast a grateful glance his way. "He was so gentle, and we talked a lot. He's lonely, and he needed a friend. I told him we could still be friends if he let me go, but he was so worried about Allan hurting me." Her face darkened. "That jerk. When I get out of here, I will break up with him. Joshua was right. I deserve better."

The police car arrived a half hour later, with PC Carol Meadham and another Detective Sergeant at the helm. After some quiet conversation, they escorted Olivia off to the police car, Tate and Clay making a promise to see her at the station when they could.

When she'd gone, Carol turned to Tate and Clay with a baleful glare. "Well, do you two want to explain yourselves? I'm sure breaking and entering isn't something the Met encouraged you to do. Neither is interfering with a crime scene. And how the hell did you know where to find her? You may have cocked this case up from the get-go for any conviction. Spill it."

Tate sighed and glanced at Clay ruefully. Time for the short story. "We were looking at the images of the chocolate moulds and found what we thought were letters engraved into the inside of them. Given they were a J, an O and an S, we figured out maybe Olivia was sending us a message and she was referring to Joshua."

Clay continued the story. "We came here, did a bit of surveillance and then…" he hesitated. "We entered the premises and did a bit of looking around. We were aware we had no warrant and that the B and E wasn't the best thing to do, but," he plastered an injured expression all over his face and Tate tried to stop from laughing at the puppy dog look, "we had concerns for her welfare and were simply doing our civic duty." He glanced at Tate. "We thought we heard her cry out for help when we called her name at the front door, didn't we? We couldn't leave her here." He lifted his chin defiantly. "And it wasn't a crime scene until we found her. So you can't blame us for interfering."

Carol's eyes narrowed. "Bullshit you heard her. She's been here two weeks and if she'd tried to make a noise, surely the neighbours would have heard?"

Clay scoffed. "Really? The street is as noisy as fuck and there's no way anyone could hear out from there. There's no one in the business above, and the area is filled with people who really don't want to get involved with anything hinky. You're taking a piss if you think anyone would have helped."

"We were probably the first people to be up close and personal to Joshua's front door." Tate offered helpfully. "He's not the sociable type." He smirked. "And from what I recall, we are official police consultants. That gives us some leeway, surely?"

They both regarded Carol innocently and it gratified Tate to see a small smile tugging at the corner of her mouth. Then she went back to being DS Officious. "I'm heading back to the station now to interview the poor woman and I'll issue an arrest warrant for Joshua when I get back there unless DI Grant has already done it. You two will need to come down and give a statement too. I expect to see you both there."

"Yes, ma'am," Tate and Clay chorused and grinned as she scowled at them.

"You two will be the death of me. I'll see you later. Now get out of here so SOCO can recover what's left of my crime scene." She gave them a withering look and walked out of the room.

"I think we just got our arses handed to us," Tate murmured in amusement. "Rick will swear at us too, no doubt."

Clay grinned. "We got the girl, and that's all that matters," he said with a satisfied smile. "The rest is semantics."

***

An hour and a half later, Tate acknowledged that they underestimated Rick's wrath. He'd pitched a fit at them for playing the cavaliers and rescuing Olivia. Then they got a full-blown lecture on police procedure, as if neither of them had a clue. Prudently, they'd kept their mouths shut. Thankfully, his nephew's ire was short-lived, and once he'd calmed down, Rick could fill in more about the case. Olivia had been taken home to recover and Rick's team had already left to arrest Joshua Bradford.

Tate wished them well. He didn't think things would go too smoothly. He toyed with his cup of disgusting coffee and contemplated running out to the corner deli for a proper cup. Perhaps a cinnamon bun too. He'd never got the bacon sandwich Clay had promised him this morning. His stomach growled angrily at that thought.

From behind his desk, Rick frowned at Tate. "Is that your bloody stomach making that awful noise? God, Clay, don't you feed my uncle?"

Clay rolled his neck from side to side and shook his head. "He's a grown man. He knows when he's hungry and when he's not."

"I didn't get that breakfast you promised me," Tate said sulkily. "Lying tosser."

Clay rolled his eyes. "For God's sake. There's a deli across the road, why don't you go buy something? You're a bitch when you get hungry."

Tate stood up. "I might do that. Order of bacon butties all round or do you fancy something sweeter?"

Rick sighed heavily. "I could do with a bacon sarnie." He regarded his coffee cup gloomily. "And a decent cup of coffee. This swill is shit."

Tate picked up his jacket and shrugged into it. The weather was bitter. His balls were frozen when he'd climbed off the back of the bike. "Righto, I'll get us some provisions. Clay, you up for a sarnie?"

Clay's face perked up. "I'd prefer a Big Mac," he said dreamily. "It's been ages since I had one of those."

Tate stared at him in disbelief. "You really want to go there? I found a wrapper in your coat pocket yesterday when we were looking for the car keys. It looked fresh to me."

"Right, but babe, that was yesterday." Clay laughed as Tate swore. "Do not stand between a man and his Big Mac."

"You're getting a bacon butty and that's it," Tate grumbled as he left the office. He worried about Clay and his passion for hamburgers. Tate tried to get him to eat healthier, but he'd never been able to convince Clay the food he loved wasn't all that good for him.

When he got back to the station and was about to go into the interview room, a voice stopped him short. It was a woman and from the sounds of it, she was reaming Clay out good and proper. Tate grinned, recognising that frosty tone.

"I'm glad you lads had fun. It's not to say I'm ungrateful you found that poor lass, but honestly Clay, did you have and your trouble-maker of a partner have to break in? You didn't think to call Rick or someone to do the legal stuff?"

Tate bristled indignantly at the words "trouble-maker of a partner." Sure, he and now Detective Chief Inspector Sheila Riley had shared a few moments of tension many years ago when they'd worked two drug cases together, and perhaps Tate had been a little gung-ho back then and not followed protocol to the letter. But to be described that way? He snorted loudly and pushed his way into the office. "Good afternoon to you too, DCI Riley. I'm not sure that's the way I'd paint myself, but you go with whatever makes you comfortable."

Clay sat perched on the corner of the desk, looking a little rattled. Sheila Riley had always had that effect on him. Tate found it amusing that a five-foot-six pixie of a woman with dark flashing eyes and skin like dark beige silk could affect Clay so.

Rick sat behind the desk grinning widely. He was enjoying this way too much, Tate thought sourly. The DCI cast an aggrieved glance at him. "Tate Williams, as I live and breathe. You know that eavesdroppers never hear good about themselves, don't you?"

Tate smirked and laid the packet containing the sandwiches on the desk, along with the tray of coffees. "Sheila, my lovely, it's been a while. I'm sorry I didn't know you were coming, I'd have brought you a bacon sandwich and coffee."

Sheila Riley glared at him. "Bullshit. You know I'm a vegetarian and detest coffee. We sat together in a police car long enough on stakeouts for you to not have forgotten that. Arsehole."

Clay's eyes widened at the insults, as did Rick's. Tate was trying to keep a straight face, but it got to be too much. He moved swiftly across the room and enfolded Sheila in a hug. "I remember, of course. You're looking good, GG."

Sheila hugged him back, her face breaking into a grin. "I told you to forget that ridiculous nickname, you heathen. God, it's great to see you."

"Should we leave you two alone?" Clay asked waspishly, his gaze darting between the two of them. "And what the fuck, Sheila? You give me the third degree but he gets a damned hug?"

Tate moved away and walked past Clay, ruffling his hair as he passed. "Ah, my man's jealous. She loves you too, baby." He passed out sandwiches and coffee to Clay and Rick.

"You wouldn't think from the way she stormed in here and handed me my arse for not doing things by the book," Clay returned. "You were there too. Picking the lock," he enunciated clearly.

Sheila tut-tutted. "Now-now lads, let's not play the blame game." She turned a fierce gaze on them both. "You both deserve to be bloody slapped. Thing is, I feel you boys would enjoy that far too much so for now my dulcet tones telling you off will have to do."

Clay grinned. "Lies, all lies, whatever Rick here has been telling you." His face grew serious. "I am grateful though you've kept things straight for us with the powers that be. I appreciate that a lot."

Sheila sighed. "Well, I can't have the dynamic duo of Butch and Sundance reflecting badly on me, can I? I'm the one who got you this gig as official police consultants."

Tate huffed. "Are you saying we're forgiven for solving the crime, rooting out the perpetrator and finding the girl, leaving you with a bona fide case to prosecute? Did I miss anything?"

Rick burst into laughter. "You had to go there, didn't you?" He stared at Tate fondly. "We know you guys did a great job. And we're happy about it even if it was rather unorthodox."

Clay stood up and threw his empty sandwich wrapper in the bin. "How is Olivia? Will we be able to see her soon, to check on how she's doing?"

Sheila nodded. "She's at home with a support officer for the rest of the day. I understand your friend Tanvi is with her. She texted the boyfriend to say she was home and safe but that they were through and not to bother coming around." Sheila smiled tightly. "I don't know exactly what went on between them, but this ordeal seems to have brought her to her senses. Another thing. She refuses to press charges against Joshua Bradford. She doesn't want to see him go to prison for trying to help her."

"It's a little weird, but I can understand that. What about Joshua?" Tate asked softly. "How is he doing?"

Sheila harrumphed. "He didn't take the arrest well, although we sent someone with the team who understands social anxiety and could work with him to get him to the station. He's in the interview room now with his lawyer his parents procured. He'll go into police custody until it's decided whether we can release him to wait for trial. The parents appear to be loaded, but a little distanced from their son as if they can't handle him." She sighed. "We're also contacting his therapist to come in. Apparently, he's been seeing someone for years now, and he insisted they come along to be with him."

"What do you think will happen?" Clay asked curiously. "I mean, it's not like he's a dangerous criminal or anything. More like a bit of a vigilante with his own sense of right and wrong. What he did wasn't right, but he did it to protect her. That must count in his favour, surely?"

Sheila tapped her nails against the desk thoughtfully. "I'd say the chances are he would be charged on the CPS's advice and sent to crown court for trial. His abilities to have detained her for a prolonged period and had the mind-set to feed and treat her so well would suggest he has some understanding of social norms and knew what he was doing. It also appears he knows the difference between right and wrong. As you say he did it to protect her, and that would suggest he knew it would be wrong to hold her."

This has been Tate's world years ago, and you could take the man out of the police force, but you couldn't remove the police training from the man. He kept up to date on things in the industry. "They could pursue the matter to proceed with what's called a victimless prosecution. It was brought in a few years back to help with domestic abuse cases where the victims wouldn't assist the police in prosecutions against their partners and are used in plenty of other scenarios like this one."

"Exactly," Sheila agreed. "It's a big deal right now because we've used resources, man-hours, money to find her, and the media appeals. The fact he drugged her isn't in his favour either. And her parents were frantically worried. So it is likely that on conviction— and I'm sure they would convict him because of him admitting to holding her at his address—that he would be dealt with sympathetically and would receive a lenient sentence. I'd expect a suspended sentence and perhaps a restraining order being put in place so it does not allow him to approach Olivia. I can't imagine they would send Joshua to prison as that would not be in the public interest."

"Wow," Clay murmured. "That's a lot of stuff right there. It'll be interesting to see how it all pans out."

"I have a couple of calls to make," Tate muttered. "No doubt Tomas will kill me if I don't tell him right away, and Clay, you may want to phone Aurelio and let him know we'd found her." He rolled his eyes. "In fact, maybe we should put out a Fetish Alley broadcast to all and sundry letting them know. Anyone got a spare carrier pigeon?"

Sheila chuckled. "Ah, the famed Alley network. You guys have done a great job making the residents feel comfortable talking to us and to you. They've always been closed mouth and your presence has made things easier for us." She smiled slyly. "Having the king lynchpin of the alley on your side is a definite bonus."

Clay bowed his head in acknowledgement. "It helps to have Relio there." He glanced over at Tate. "I suggest we make our way home and make the calls from there. They'll probably go on for a while."

Tate was more than ready to go home and spread the good news. In today's time of violence and politics, it was something they could all do with. He felt sorry for Joshua. He'd been trying to protect a friend, even if he chose a shitty way to do it. "Is it possible to observe the interview?" Tate asked hopefully. "I'd like to see what Joshua has to say."

Sheila sighed. "I s'pose. It's down the hall. Interview room two. This is one of the new rooms so it has a one-way window. I'll let Rick keep you up to date on what happens next." She waved a hand as if conjuring them out of her sight and Tate and Clay walked down to the empty observation room wedged between the two interview rooms.

Joshua sat in a chair, a glass of water by his side and an unopened sandwich on the table. He was hunched over, looking fragile, and Tate's heart went out to him. Here was a young man who'd tried to do the right thing by doing the wrong thing.

Tate didn't recognise the constable conducting the interview or the slim woman who sat next to Joshua, leaning in occasionally to say something to him. No doubt his lawyer.

"Thanks for answering my questions so far, Joshua," the constable, a dark-skinned man in his thirties, said with a warm smile. "Let me recap. You encouraged Olivia to come and have a drink with you at your home. You then gave Olivia a drink with some sedative in it to help her sleep. Then you carried her into her room, the one you created especially for her. And that's where she was all the time she was missing for the nearly two weeks. Is that correct?"

Joshua sat stock still playing his fingers on the table to an unheard beat. Finally, he nodded. "I suppose."

"Did Olivia ask to go home? Did she tell you wanted to leave?"

The woman next to Joshua rolled her eyes. "DC Booth, you've asked that question already, and he's given you an answer. Do we have to repeat all this?"

"Miss Lang, yes, I do. It's my job to find out exactly how Joshua saw all this playing out and whether he understood what he was doing."

Miss Lang gave an exasperated snort. "As his lawyer, I'm not sure repeating the questions will do any good." She tapped an impatient finger on the table. "His therapist will be here soon, and you can talk to him too. Obviously, Joshua's medical and psychological history needs to be taken into consideration, but I doubt they'll tell you much, given patient confidentiality."

DC Booth inclined his head respectfully. "I understand that, Miss. Lang. I'm almost finished with Joshua and then he can see his parents. I understand they are waiting to talk to him. And we will consider anything the therapist shares with us."

He turned to Joshua again. "Did Olivia say at any time she wanted to go home?"

Joshua fiddled with his sleeve, enraptured in the white buttons. DC Booth waited patiently.

"She said she would always be my friend, but I had to let her go home," Joshua finally muttered fretfully. "I explained to her that wasn't wise, and she needed to stay with me until Allan gave up and let her go. She shouted at me and I left the room. I tried to explain what I was doing for her, but she got mad."

DC Booth nodded thoughtfully. "How did you think her boyfriend would give up? Did you think perhaps he'd think she'd left him and he'd find another girlfriend?"

Joshua looked up, his eyes finally reflecting emotion. "Yes, I thought he would leave her then I could take her home. I always meant to take her home. I'd never hurt her." He smiled suddenly, his face wistful. "We had pizza together and watched a whole series of Supernatural. Both of us love that programme."

He fell silent, playing with a button on his polo shirt. "Will I be able to see Olivia soon and see how she is?"

DC Booth smiled at him kindly. "I don't think that will be possible Joshua. Let's see how things go." He glanced at his watch. "I think that's it for now. Your parents are here to talk to you and tell you what happens next. Interview ended at eighteen fifteen pm."

Tate and Clay walked out of the observation room.

"Time to go home. I need a brandy," Clay muttered as he rubbed the back of his neck. "It's been an eventful day and I could do with putting my feet up and watching some mindless telly."

"I concur," Tate said. "First, we have some calls to make. Then the rest of the evening is ours. Come on, hotshot. Let's do this."

Chapter 12

Aurelio stared out of the window in his office, taking in the scene below. The alley was alive with people as the annual Christmas Fair played out. Stalls lined the narrow-cobbled alleys as far as the eye could see, decked out in twinkling fairy lights, flickering candles and Chinese lanterns. People milled around the tables dressed for the cold, and he chuckled at the sight of a large St Andrews Cross festooned with tiny twinkling Santa lights.

"Only in the Alley," he murmured to himself. "I suppose I should join the fun." He turned as his mobile rang once and his heart leapt. Then the phone went silent. Someone had thought better of it.

Perhaps it was Tomas.

While they had been speaking when Tomas was abroad, the conversations had been awkward and uncomfortable. Aurelio knew his young man was grieving about the loss of his friend. He wanted to be there for him but Tomas had refused all offers of support. The one good thing that had happened was that Tomas was due home in the next couple of days. Then Aurelio meant to sit him down and have a heart to heart about their mutual expectations.

He knew he'd fallen for Tomas, badly. The first time he'd seen the brash and sexy man with the prickly attitude, Aurelio had known he wanted to get to know him better. Despite their age difference, Tomas was wise beyond his years, his past the trigger for him growing up faster than typical.

"But he is so damned stubborn and used to being on his own," Aurelio muttered as he picked up his phone to find out who the caller had been.

Clay Mortimer.

A surge of warm affection replaced the initial disappointment that it hadn't been his lover. Clay, an ex-lover, was a man Aurelio both respected and loved as a friend even if he had an annoying fiancé who resembled a lithe, caustic black panther. Tate Williams was the perfect match for Clay, and Clay was besotted with the man, but did he have to choose a wise-cracking, dark humoured and irritating individual?

"No wonder he and Tomas get on so well together," Aurelio grumbled as he dialled Clay back. "They're chips off the same block. And trying to settle Tomas was like trying to put a collar on a spitting cobra."

And settle Tomas was what Aurelio wanted to do. Give Tomas someone to rely on, someone to trust, someone to... love.

Clay picked up almost immediately. "Relio? You doing well?"

Aurelio sat on the edge of his desk, watching the festivities below. "I am well my friend. I am watching a man getting mock flogged on a cross covered with twinkling Santa Clauses, and a woman in a latex cat suit administering the whip. Welcome to my life."

Clay laughed. "The perfect evening for you then. I needed to call you and give the good news. We found Olivia, and she's safe and sound."

Aurelio closed his eyes and said a heartfelt prayer. "Thank God. That is the best news I've had today. Where was she found?"

He listened in disbelief as Clay outlined the events leading up to Olivia's discovery. When he'd finished, Aurelio sat down behind his desk and scowled. "I understand your sympathy for the young man who was only trying to help, but we cannot allow him to think he is above the law. It has caused her parents' distress, as it has many people in the Alley, especially Tomas. It has worried him sick."

"And I'm sure they'll deal with him fairly, Relio. This kid has some psychological history which needs taking into account. The police has ways of dealing with these sorts of situations."

"Hmm." Relio wasn't convinced. "I must take your word for that. Have you called Tomas to tell him yet?"

"Tate is on the phone as we speak, trying to get a hold of him. Tomas's phone keeps going to messaging so I assume he's got no signal where he is, or he's busy."

Aurelio wondered where he might be. Probably sorting out the funeral for Valentin and had put his phone on silent. "He will be pleased to hear the news. Especially after his time spent in Lithuania. It hasn't been a pleasant trip. Thank you for letting me know, my friend."

"Anytime. Tate and I are planning to go see Olivia when things settle down, make sure she's doing all right. Oh, I called Tanvi too. She's over the moon and promised to tell everyone else in the Alley the good news. No doubt it will spread like wildfire." Clay sounded amused. "I feel she's quite an institution down there. Well-liked."

"She is," Aurelio confirmed. "Tanvi is a lovely woman and takes in many stray goats."

Clay guffawed. "Goats? Stray sheep, Relio. You slay me sometimes."

Aurelio huffed. "Goats can stray too. I do not see what is so funny." He had a fleeting thought of Tomas giggling at his poor word choices too and a pang of nostalgia clutched his chest and wouldn't let go.

Come home, Tomas. Please come home.

"Anyway, I'd better be off. Tate's cooking dinner and he's moaning it's going cold." Clay murmured something under his breath and Aurelio heard a growled response from Tate. "We'll catch up next week, yeah? Perhaps if Tomas is back you and he can come over for dinner? It would be nice to see you here again for a change."

Aurelio sighed. "I have no idea when he'll be back," he confessed. "But absolutely, if he is, I would love to visit. It has been a while."

He said his goodbyes and set his mobile on the desk, staring at it, willing it to ring, to hear Tomas was coming home. He started when a voice from the open doorway him intruded on his thoughts. A beloved voice that sent a thrill through him.

"Staring at it like that will not change anything, *mano meilė*. Is it me you were waiting for?"

Aurelio stood up slowly, feeling the smile on his face widen with each second. "It is always you, *tesoro*." He left the desk to greet the man standing in the doorway. Tomas looked thinner and tired, his face pale, his cheekbones standing out. His beautiful blue eyes were haunted and dark shadows encircled them. Tomas lugged the backpack off his shoulders and hurried toward Aurelio, grasping him in a fierce embrace. Tomas smelt of pine trees and whisky, and the welcome scent of familiarity.

"I'm so pleased you are home, *caro*," Aurelio murmured into Tomas's sweaty hair, the tangle of it tickling his nose.

"I am pleased to be home," Tomas whispered, his voice trembling. "I missed you, Relio. So much."

Aurelio tilted Tomas's chin and claimed his lips in a tender kiss. Tomas made a soft sound in his throat and hugged Aurelio tighter. His mouth claimed Aurelio's desperately and Aurelio welcomed it. He needed Tomas to take what he needed, needed to show his man how much of Aurelio's heart he owned.

Finally, they drew apart, their cocks hard against each other but Aurelio was content to simply hold his lover. There was time for lovemaking later. Tomas seemed to need nothing but closeness.

"Come, sit down, and tell me about everything," he murmured, steering Tomas over the couch in the corner. "I have heard some of it in pieces, but now it's time you tell me everything. Are you hungry? I can get you something to eat if you like?"

Tomas shook his head tiredly as he collapsed onto the couch. "No, I ate on the plane. It was crappy food, but it served a purpose." He managed a glimmer of a grin. "All I want to do is sit here with you for a while. And I want to rejoice because they found Olivia. Tate got hold of me and the news made me happy."

He snuggled into Aurelio's side, his soft breaths rhythmic in the quiet of the room. Aurelio closed his eyes, relishing the warm body in his arms, waiting patiently for Tomas to talk.

Tomas was home. Nothing else mattered.

It was almost ten minutes later when Tomas spoke. "Valentin's funeral is arranged for next week." He cleared his throat. "I wondered if you'd come with me back home for it? I would like you by my side."

Aurelio's heart stuttered. Tomas wanted him there? Wild stallions would not keep him away. "Of course, *caro*. If that is what you want."

"Thanks," Tomas whispered. There was silence again. Then, "Val had a brain tumour. It got worse in the last few months and finally, they sent him to a hospice. We all knew he didn't have long. They had prepared him for it, as much as you can when facing something like that."

"I am so sorry, *cuore mio*." Aurelio hugged him closer. "It is a terrible thing to suffer and watch someone you know battle it. It tears your soul apart."

"You say that like you've had experience?" Tomas shifted to look at Aurelio.

Aurelio nodded. "I think we all know someone who has lost a loved one. For me, it was an old football friend. We used to play together in the team until he got sick with cancer. Watching him die was heart breaking. So I understand what you've been through."

"Val and I were not only friends, but we were also once lovers as teenagers." Tomas rubbed his eyes. "His foster family was like a family to me, while I was on the streets. They were poor, and they couldn't take me in, having one extra mouth to feed was too much, but Val and I would play football in the streets, and steal smokes behind the old concrete sheds that doubled as a shelter for the homeless. I have kept in touch with them all these years and it was them who called me to say Val was asking for me."

There was a watery sniff from somewhere beneath Aurelio's chin. "I saw him every time I went home. When I saw him last time, about a year ago, he said nothing. I noticed he was tired and forgetful but when I asked him about it he laughed and said he was fine. Stupid man. I could have been there with him, helping him through it. Instead, I arrived there only to find him wasted away and yet still, he had this smile that dazzled you, made you feel as if he was on top of the world." Tomas was crying freely now, tears rolling down his hollow cheeks. Aurelio hugged him close, stroking his back and murmuring words of comfort in his ears.

"He did not want you to suffer with him, Tomas. His only thought was saving you from pain. The most important thing is that he asked for you when he was near the end. He needed you then, and this was his journey to take." Aurelio kissed the top of Tomas's head. "And we will honour him when we go to his last resting place. I will give thanks to him for being a friend to you, and you will remember his love and his friendship. And that will give you the courage to continue without him."

Tomas sniffed and Aurelio reached inside his trouser pocket and drew out a pristine handkerchief. "Here, dry your eyes, *amore mio*. Then perhaps, if you feel like it, we can go down into the Alley and walk along the stalls. There is a party going on down there which might help you forget for a little while."

Tomas wiped his eyes then blew his nose in the hankie. "I saw that as I came in. It looks festive with all the Christmas lights."

"Well, Christmas is only a few weeks away." Aurelio knew it was Tomas's favourite season. He had great expectations of the club being kitted out like something out of Deck the Halls. Aurelio wasn't one for the season but if it made his Tomas happy, he'd endure it.

Tomas snuggled closer. "I know I can be a bit of a bitch, Relio. I'm sorry. Trusting people is difficult for me."

Aurelio stroked his fingers through Tomas' hair, loving the happy sounds his man made. "I understand that. Your childhood wasn't exactly a bed of lilies, and you have had to fight hard to get where you are."

Tomas laughed softly. "It's a bed of roses, *mano meilė*. Not lilies." He looked up at Aurelio, his blue eyes serious. "Growing up in foster care as I did, in a country that didn't really care about us, hardened me. It toughened me up. The authorities were not good to people like me, their lost children, and we fought hard to keep out of their way or they'd brutalise us. We were nothing but scum to them, playthings to hurt and sometimes even kill. When I found Val's family, I finally felt like someone wanted me. When they fell on hard times and were struggling to make ends meet, I left, and came to London. I met this woman called Elle, who was a master hacker. She taught me everything I know."

"She must have been an interesting woman, *caro*." Aurelio kissed Tomas' brow softly. "Where is she now?"

Tomas sighed. "She married a man who whisked her off to Monte Carlo. We still keep in touch occasionally."

Aurelio loved hearing about Tomas's life, getting to know his young man for the wonderful person that hid beneath the snark and prickly nature. He wanted to spend the rest of his life finding out more and sharing stories of his own.

"I was fortunate," Aurelio murmured. "I had a wonderful childhood, a loving upbringing by parents who loved me. I played a game I adored with people who became good friends. Then there is Clay, who will always be someone I treasure in my life."

"How did you two meet?" Tomas asked curiously.

Aurelio chuckled. "We met in Turkey when I was there for a Premiership game. He was on leave from the army. After the game, there was this party and the wife of one the other players invited him. I saw this man across the room and thought he was magnificent, all broody and tough. I carried my drink over and bumped into him on purpose, drenching him in red wine." Aurelio laughed at the memory of dismay on Clay's face as his pristine white shirt had become soaked with the ruby liquid. "I convinced him to let me help him clean it up." He shrugged his shoulders. "My allure was such that we fucked in the upstairs bedroom and it went from there."

"Do you still have feelings for Clay?" Tomas's voice muffled as he pressed his lips against Aurelio's chest, seeking the bare skin beneath his shirt which had mysteriously opened. Aurelio hitched a breath as Tomas nipped lightly at a nipple.

"*Tesoro*, not like before. Now he is a great friend, and he always loved Tate, even when we were together. No man could have lived up to that irritating individual in Clay's mind."

"He can be an arsehole," Tomas agreed as he looked up at Aurelio, wicked eyes shining with mischief. "But he is a good friend to me too. They work well together, those two."

Aurelio agreed. "Like you and I, Tomas. My beautiful boy." His lips found Tomas's, who opened his mouth eagerly and Aurelio sighed into it as they kissed passionately. When they came up for air, Aurelio gently moved Tomas aside. He needed a distraction, so he didn't pull Tomas into the bedroom right that minute. His man needed a touch of something festive, something celebratory and later that night, there would be a time for making love.

"Come, let's get you a jacket and go downstairs. I promise to buy you a large mug of mulled wine and one of those awful pretzel things you like so much." He winked. "Then we can come home and cuddle up in bed and I can tell you how much I missed you."

Tomas laughed, and the sound pulled at Aurelio's heartstrings. "You must think I'm terribly easy. I will insist on the wine, the pretzel and a packet of roasted chestnuts."

Aurelio wrinkled his nose in distaste. He abhorred roasted chestnuts. "If that is what you wish." He stood up and motioned to Tomas to come with him. "Come. Let's get warm and visit our friends. Cleaver and Tanvi have missed you, as has the rest of the staff. I think sometimes if I was the one who went away, they would not be as concerned."

He started to move toward the hallway and the closet, and Tomas caught his arm. "Relio."

"Yes?"

Tomas's eyes shone but there were no tears this time. "I know I can be difficult, but seeing Val like that, knowing he was not long for this world... I realised something." He hesitated. "I need to acknowledge when I have good things in my life and you, you are the best thing I have. I don't tell you enough, but I wanted you to know."

Aurelio lost his breath. "You are the world to me too. I am a lucky man to have you. And hearing those words from you too means everything to me."

They looked at each other for a few seconds then Tomas nudged him. "Look at us, getting soft. Let's go out there and say hello. We're missing the party."

He dashed off to fetch his coat and Aurelio followed him, knowing something amazing had happened. It was too early for the L-word. Tomas would probably still be skittish. It seemed though that the time he'd had to think had given him a new appreciation for Aurelio and he could only hope it continued.

Because life without Tomas was too painful to contemplate.

Chapter 13

"I am not putting on a fucking elf suit and giving the kids at the shelter a show," Tate growled as he threw one of the couch cushions flew across the room, hitting Jax squarely in the face. "I don't care how much you beg me."

Archie barked, his little tail wagging excitedly as he chased the path of the cushion across the room.

"Way to go, T, throwing something at the blind man in the room," Jax chortled as he cast a mischievous glance in Clay's direction. "Dare, did you see that? He attacked me when I was defenceless. What are you going to do about it?"

Dare's broad shoulders rolled in a shrug. "Babe, I will sit right here and finish eating my pigs in blankets." He popped another one of the delicious goodies he'd made into his mouth. The tray was laden with snacks and fruit. "You can take care of this one yourself." He grinned at Clay and sneakily took a snack off the tray and fed it to Archie.

"Ooh, burn," Tate said gleefully as he too took about his tenth bacon rolled treat off the tray on the centre table. Clay was sure the man would explode soon. Given Tate had already eaten half a dozen small pasties and a gallon of mulled wine. "And you've never been defenceless in your life, Baby Bird."

"Will you stop with that stupid nickname?" Jax snarked as he threw the cushion back in Tate's general direction. "I thought we agreed never to use it again." Archie was going crazy trying to get the flying missile, his bark sharp and loud. Clay cringed at the chaos.

"Archie, enough," he commanded. "That sound goes right through me." The dog sat down, tail wagging, and gave Clay a dopey grin.

"You agreed we shouldn't use it again," Tate pointed out as he sat back in his chair and belched happily. "I never did." He reached out to scratch Archie between the ears.

"And on that childish note, can we call a truce?" Clay murmured, looking around at his family fondly. "You two are bloody terrible when you get together." He caught Dare's gaze and the two men acknowledged their spouses' behaviour with a rueful nod.

"He started it," Both Jax and Tate exclaimed in tandem.

Clay watched the cushion being tossed back and forth, Archie once again entering the fray. Dare wisely leaned back and ignored the tomfoolery. He seemed preoccupied with watching the music videos on the Christmas channel of the telly. Jax's choice of music. The young man was a sucker for all things Christmas. And today was Christmas Day, so he was making the most of it.

Clay did too, but for him, it was about having a family. His parents, Percy and Angela were still living in Surrey, but they'd chosen to do a world cruise this year over Christmas. Not that Clay saw them a lot. He Skyped and when he was in the area, he'd pop in for tea or something stronger. Tate's parents had died many years ago, and he only had Lucy and Rick. They were visiting later today to drop off Christmas presents and have some eggnog.

He'd invited Aurelio and Tomas, but they'd declined. Aurelio was taking Tomas to Switzerland for the festive season. It was on Tomas's bucket list. The younger man needed a distraction after his friend's funeral.

Jax, and by extension, his doting boyfriend, Dare, had come into Clay and Tate's lives and brought with them a whole new facet to their family. Tate was like a big brother to Jax, while Clay served as somewhat of a father figure. It was strangely fulfilling and something Clay hadn't ever thought he'd experience. He'd never been one for children, and luckily, Tate felt the same. But having Jax in their lives added something new and cherished to their relationship.

Watching the camaraderie between his small family unit, in their home, surrounded by a six-foot Christmas tree lit up with white and gold lights, a crackling log fire and a myriad of presents under the tree, was overwhelming. Having Archie as part of the family was an unexpected if noisy, bonus.

"Hey, old man, you look as if you're spacing out." Jax's amused voice broke into his thoughts and the cushion flew across to hit Clay in the face.

"Hey. Leave me out of your bro fights," he exclaimed. Clay took the offending cushion and smugly tucked it behind him in his chair. "I was thinking it might be time to open the presents." Archie gave a huff and lay down at his feet, his fun time stopped.

Dare had been flicking idly through the TV channels and he called out as something caught his interest. "Hey, guys? There's something on the telly about Olivia."

They all turned to see the screen and watch the news broadcast. The newscaster was in front of a courthouse and she turned to watch as a group of people left the court.

"The disappearance of Olivia du Preez was solved when she was found unharmed in the house belonging to a young man called Joshua Bradford. This was no ordinary disappearance. Joshua claimed he had falsely imprisoned Olivia to save her from an abusive boyfriend. It was because of the concerted efforts of the London police force and two private consultants, who have asked to remain unnamed, that led the police to Olivia's place of capture and resulted in her being freed.

While the full details are still being closely guarded from what we gathered at the hearing today, Mr Bradford received a suspended sentence. For how long, we don't know yet. He has to adhere to a restraining order that he will not get close to Ms du Preez."

The reporter stopped talking and listened carefully to her earpiece. "I'm receiving a news flash that Olivia du Preez has challenged the restraining order and is seeking to overturn it. What a strange development in this already strange story. It seems to hold shades of the Patty Hearst story where the victim sympathised with their kidnapper. We'll bring you more news as soon as we have it."

The broadcast skipped to something about fishing rights in the French Channel. Dare muted the sound with a scowl. "Fucking Brexit. I'm sick and tired of hearing about it."

"You and me both," Clay murmured. "Well, that went exactly as Sheila Riley said it would. Suspended sentence and a restraining order. I'm not surprised Olivia is trying to stop the order. When Tate and I saw her two weeks ago, she told us she had every intention of remaining friends with Joshua. She's a spirited young lady. I'm sure she'll get it sorted."

Tate tossed a grape into his mouth. "Yeah, she seemed pretty determined." He shook his head at a drooling Archie whose gaze was drawn to the platter of food." Nuh-huh. Not for you, pup. Grapes aren't good for doggies." He reached over and plucked a cocktail sausage off. "You can have this instead." Tate threw it to Archie who caught it and munched away happily

"It's fascinating," Jax said, his eyes shining. "From a psychological perspective, it's almost Stockholm Syndrome but not quite. And Joshua sounds like an interesting person to observe." Clay didn't miss the tone in the young man's voice at the same time he loved the way Jax threw such terms around with ease. His continuing education was paying off, as was his passion about their halfway house. It was running well with no further traumas, a fact for which Clay was grateful.

"So are we going to open presents or what?" Tate demanded impatiently. "I have a pile here with my name on it." The presents had already been sorted and given to each of them by an eager Jax. "I'm looking forward to opening the one Clay got me." He smirked. "The new leather jacket I fancied."

Clay rolled his eyes. "Don't be so sure. That was an expensive jacket and who says you're worth it?" He'd purchased it, of course, because his man was tough to buy presents for and Tate had fallen so in love with the item. A little uncertainty worked wonders though.

"So let's do it," Jax said, filling up his wine glass with more warmed mulled wine. "All at once." He smirked. "We opened our presents to each other at home this morning. He was like a kid when he woke up and I couldn't resist his little eager face."

Dare rolled his eyes. "Jax, you were looking in the mirror when you saw that eager face."

Jax laughed and began ripping the paper off his gifts. That was the catalyst for everyone else to get down to it. The room filled with the sound of ripping paper, shouts of delight and Archie's yipping as he joined in, even without having a clue what was going on. Clay remembered he'd bought something for the pup and he reached under the tree to draw it out.

"Here you go, Arch. You didn't think we'd forgotten you, did you?" He laid the brightly wrapped parcel down on the floor and chuckled when Archie sniffed it and began tearing the paper with his little teeth.

Jax gave a squeal of delight. "He's too cute. Dare, we need to get a puppy too. Oh my God, babe. Look at this." Jax drew out a new laptop from within a bunch of torn paper. His old one had been giving him issues for a while and he'd been promising to get himself a new one, but it hadn't happened. Clay and Tate had decided they'd make it happen. "Wow, this is really fancy, it's got all the updated accessibility functions and extra ones to boot." His blue eyes looked over at Clay and then Tate. "Thanks, guys. This is awesome. My old one was getting a little temperamental."

Clay nodded to another wrapped box. "That one's for both of you."

Jax pushed the box over to Dare. "You open this one," he commanded. Dare ripped the paper off to reveal a small hamper covered in cellophane. "This looks interesting," he muttered. "I have a bad feeling about this one."

Jax helped him take the cellophane off and then both men stood staring down at the basket of goodies Clay and Tate had put together from Lewd Foods.

"Oh wow," Jax said in awe. "Look at this stuff." He picked up the rimming sugar and gave a throaty chuckle. "This is epic. Look, Dare, something for you too. Cemen dip."

Dare looked over at Clay and Tate with a grin. "This is most unusual," he murmured. "Thanks a lot. I'm sure we'll get some fun out of all these treats." He picked up the packet of Cock Flavoured Soup mix and raised a sardonic eyebrow. "I'm sure I can find a use for this."

Jax chortled loudly. "I love this stuff. Thanks, guys. Tate, time to open your present."

Tate reached for the gaudily wrapped gift bag and reached a hand in to hold up a pair of navy-blue boxer trunks. He scowled. "So whose idea was this then?" Across the groin area was emblazoned "Property of Godzilla."

Jac went into a fit of the giggles as Dare chuckled and looked on in fond amusement. "Who do you think?" Dare murmured. "Check out the other pair."

Tate reached into the festive box and pulled out a red pair that had, "It's not going to spank itself," written across the backside. Clay couldn't help himself, the look of disbelief on Tate's face was precious.

"Oh yeah, they have your number," Clay said, not even trying to stifle his laughter.

"There is something else in the box." Jax motioned to it. "Dig deeper."

Tate rummaged around the box and finally produced another slimmer box. He heaved a sigh as he stared at it in suspicion. "This isn't going to blow up in my face or have something jump out, is it?" he asked warily.

Dare shook his head, the grin on his face growing wider. "Naw. I promise you it's safe to open."

Tate's face, when he opened the gift, was a picture. His beaming smile lit the room up. "A Kindle Oasis," he said excitedly. "How did you guys know I wanted one of these?" He busied himself looking at his present.

"Oh, a little bird might have mentioned it," said Jax, with a wink at Clay. "Glad you like it."

Archie had finished tearing apart his present and was now lying happily eating the large chew bone they'd bought him. *That's one way to keep him quiet*, Clay thought.

He'd delayed opening his presents and now he began trying to get the paper of them without tearing it. It was something he did, not wanting to ruin something someone had taken time doing. When he saw what Jax and Dare had given him, his eyes stung and he blinked back the tears threatening to fall. "This is beautiful." There were two gifts in his box. One was a framed picture of him and Tate standing by the bike, windswept and natural, smiling into each other's eyes. It was an unguarded moment and one Clay remembered but didn't think had been captured on film.

"Dare snapped that when we went to Devon for the weekend, remember? You guys took the bike and Dare and I followed in the car. It's such a fabulous picture of you both, we thought you should have it. Now open the other one."

Clay picked up the long box and removed the top. He had a feeling he knew what it was from the branding on the box, but when he saw the beautiful Hugo Boss Rose Gold rollerball pen lying against black velvet, it was even lovelier than he'd imagined. "This is the one I saw months ago and said I'd like. I guess we have a lot of little birds with big mouths in this family." He looked at Tate who smiled at him. "Thank you both. This is a wonderful gift."

Jax shrugged. "Well, you said Tate was always stealing yours and then he says they're his, so now he can't do that."

Tate was tugging fiercely at the paper around the large box Clay had put under the tree for him. When he finally got the white gift box open, he gave a yell of triumph and delight.

"Hah, I knew it." He drew a soft leather jacket out from the box. "This is perfect, thanks, babe. It's the exact one I wanted." He held it up excitedly. "My precious," he crooned in a passable Gollum voice. "Come to me, my precious."

And now it was Dare's turn. Both Clay and Tate turned to watch the man's face as he opened the large box then frowned when he pulled another large gift-wrapped box out. "Okaaay," he said doubtfully. He got that one open and found yet another smaller box inside. Tate was grinning and Jax was giggling.

"It's the gift that keeps on giving," Clay remarked dryly. "It wasn't my idea."

Five boxes later Dare finally got to the envelope secreted inside the last narrow box. He drew it out and opened it with Jax craning over his shoulder. Clay had never seen Dare speechless before.

"Well, what is it?" Jax demanded to know.

"I can't accept this, guys," Dare said, his eyes wide. "I mean, it must have been really expensive."

"It's our gift," Tate said with a grin. "One you can both enjoy because you've both worked so damned hard getting the shelter off the ground."

"What the fuck is it?" Jax said impatiently. "I can't see so well from here."

"It's a trip to Venice with flights and accommodation and a chance to see Chef Mario Marchesi up close and personal in a special cooking class."

"Ohhh." Jax nudged Dare on his shoulder all the while shooting an affectionate glance at Clay and Tate. "That's the one you drool over when he comes on the telly? The hot Italian guy that gives you a boner?"

"He does not give me a boner," Dare said hotly. "Yes, he's fit, but it's his cooking I enjoy."

"I beg to differ," Jax said wickedly. "I think I might have been the lucky recipient of your said boner once or twice when you've come to bed after watching his show."

"Hell, Jax," Dare hissed, his face turning pink. "Have you no bloody decorum?"

"I'm thinking not," Clay muttered as Tate fell in laughter beside him. "Anyway, boners aside, we wanted to give you both something to enjoy and remember. We knew you liked this man—although not as much as Jax seems to think you do—and it made sense. When you're ready to go, you let me know and I'll get it all sorted."

Dare stood and gave Clay a hug then did the same to Tate. "Thank you," he murmured, still sounding overwhelmed. Now they were all standing, slapping each other's backs and hugging as they gave thanks for the gifts. Archie took part too, giving licks all around.

"Wait a minute," Jax said after they'd sat back down and poured more mulled wine and opened the eggnog, Archie comfortably snuggled on his lap as Jax's fingers stroked him. "We're missing a present. Tate, where's yours for Clay?" He cast an accusing glance at Clay's fiancé who raised his eyebrows.

"He gets to bed me every night, what more does he need?" Tate scoffed.

Clay had been so caught up with everyone else he hadn't even thought about Tate's gift for him. "Not quite every night, honey," he mocked gently. "And yes, where's my present?"

Tate sighed dramatically and stood up to wander over to the cabinet on the side of the room. He opened the door, scrabbled around then took out a shiny gold-wrapped parcel that looked like a book. Clay wondered if it was the new Clive Cussler he'd wanted.

Tate handed it to Clay. "I hope you like this," he said gruffly. "I never know quite what to get you."

Clay peeled the paper off slowly and dropped it to the floor. It was a book, a slim volume of images, and the most surprising thing of all was Tate's name on the cover.

Tate Williams - Symphony in Street Art

Clay paged through it, seeing images he recognised in full, beautiful glossy colour. Tate's graffiti art reflected on every page, together with a short description of the image and a personal note from Tate himself.

"Babe, this is incredible," Clay got out, fighting past the lump in his throat. "How did you do this? I had no idea."

"Read the dedication," Tate said quietly.

Clay opened the book to one of the pages in the front of the book, and the lump in his throat grew larger as he read the text aloud.

I dedicate this to my soulmate, Clay. The man who lights up my life in more ways than I can count and keeps me grounded.

Clay stopped and swallowed before finding his breath and carrying on.

Art reflects the artist's mood and emotions. It's a song from the soul which pours forth and allows the observer to see the artist in a new light. Sometimes people cross your path and have a profound effect on the life we creatives want to portray. Sometimes we may not appreciate these individuals because they make us face things we'd rather forget. They force us to confront the demons we hide inside and to cast them out or at the very least, teach us to understand WE have control, not the demons.

I have collected this art over a long period and it reflects varying moods and influences present in my life. Some are dark and disturbing, others are light and uplifting. And through it all, Clay has been there for me, and I can't thank him enough for helping me get to the place I am now.

"If I know what love is, it is because of you."—Hermann Hesse

"Jesus, Tate, I can't even..." Clay's voice trailed off as he looked up at his fiancé. "I knew you had photos of your work squirrelled away but how did this happen?" He raised the book. Jax was smiling, clutching onto Dare who looked as emotional as Clay felt. Jax's big, burly boyfriend was a sucker for anything romantic.

"Well, you know I always take a picture of my art once I've finished it. I collated all the images from over the years and put them in sequence, adding a little note where it was taken and what I felt. Then I sent the rough draft over to a publisher who declined to publish it, but who had another publishing house in mind they thought might do it. It's a small, independent press in Scotland. They said it was something unique, and they liked it, so they popped over a contract and," Tate shrugged, "I checked it out with Rick's solicitor—did you know he has a solicitor for all his stuff?—they made a few changes, the publisher agreed, and they produced this book in time for Christmas." He gave a wry grin. "I don't think it'll make a bestseller list anywhere because I'm shit at branding and stuff, and I hate social media but all I wanted was one copy. For you."

His gaze grew anxious. "You don't think it's a stupid idea, do you? Because I—" His words were cut off as Clay reached him with two long strides and claimed Tate's mouth as if they were the only two people in the room. Clay's heart burst that his Tate, his contrary, cynical and wise-cracking Tate, had gone to all this for him, kept it secret, so he could send him a message of such profound love that Clay doubted anyone could top.

"Aww, look at the 'rents," Jax stage whispered, his voice sounding choked. "One day that'll be you and me, Candyman."

Clay was still being thoroughly kissed, but he thought he heard the other couple exit the room, shutting the door softly behind them. No doubt going to do some making out of their own, Clay thought in a daze.

Finally, they drew apart, both needing to come up for air. Clay nestled his cheek in Tate's hair. "That is the best present anyone has ever given me," he murmured. "Honestly, babe, it was such a surprise and I'm so proud of you. You're published now. That's something I never thought I'd hear myself say."

"It's not about being published." Tate drew away, his hazel eyes filled with emotion. "It's about telling you how I feel, and how important you are to me. I know I'm shit at that so this was an easier way of getting that message across."

"I never doubted it." Clay moved and regarded the snoring dog on the couch. "We have a family of our own, with those two men through there and this chap." He leaned down and brushed a finger across Archie's fur as the dog wriggled in delight, "And I can't think of anywhere else in life I'd rather be."

They helped themselves to more eggnog then sat down on the couch, snuggling into one each other, watching the flames of the fire leap and dance in the hearth.

"Do you think they'll be back?" Tate said. "Or will we have to go find them?" He wrinkled his nose. "As long as they aren't christening our bed. I'm good with whatever they're up to."

"They'll be back," Clay confirmed. "The roast goose is still in the oven and from the scent wafting over, it needs to come out. Dare will be here any minute to check his precious bird."

Tate gave a satisfied snicker and sipped his drink.

As Clay held Tate close, smelling his scent and feeling the throb of his heart against his own, and the warmth of strong arms wrapped around his neck, he truly believed he'd never had a better Christmas.

ABOUT THE AUTHOR

The 'Official' stuff

Susan writes steamy, sexy, and fun contemporary romance stories, some suspenseful, some gritty and dark, and she hopes, always entertaining. She's also Editor-in-Chief at Divine Magazine, an online LGBTQ e-zine, and a member of The Society of Authors, the Writers Guild of Great Britain, and the Authors Guild in the U.S.

Susan is also an award-winning screenplay writer, with scripts based on two of her own published works. *Sight Unseen* has garnered no less than five awards to date, and her TV pilot, *Reel Life*, based on her debut novel, *Cassandra by Starlight*, was also a winner at the Oaxaca Film Fest.

The 'Unofficial' stuff

Susan loves going to the theatre, live music concerts (especially if it's her man-crush Adam Lambert), walks in the countryside, a good G and T, lazing away afternoons reading a good book, and watching re-runs of *Silent Witness*.

Her chequered past includes stories like being mistaken for a prostitute in the city of Johannesburg, being chased by a rhino on a dusty Kenyan road, getting kicked out of a youth club for being a bad influence (she encouraged free thinking), and having an aunt who was engaged to Cliff Richard.

Connect with Susan:

website: authorsusanmacnicol.com
facebook: Author-Susan-Mac-Nicol
twitter: SusanMacNicol7
instagram: susiemax77
linkedin: susanmacnicol

www.BOROUGHSPUBLISHINGGROUP.com

If you enjoyed this book, please write a review. Our authors appreciate the feedback, and it helps future readers find books they love. We welcome your comments and invite you to send them to info@boroughspublishinggroup.com. Follow us on Facebook, Twitter and Instagram, and be sure to sign up for our newsletter for surprises and new releases from your favorite authors.

Are you an aspiring writer? Check out www.boroughspublishinggroup.com/submit and see if we can help you make your dreams come true.